"I'm not ashamed of my poetry."

Shauna's voice was low. "But I told you before, it's *personal*. That's just the way I feel. I can't help it."

Michael gave a brief, bitter laugh. "No, I don't suppose you can. Any more than I can help—" He stopped.

"Any more than you can help . . . what?"

"Shauna, my whole life has been a matter of seeing what I wanted, going after it and getting it. I never learned how to wait for something to be given instead of taking it."

"But you've said you always get what you want."

"Not quite always."

The message she read in his eyes made her heart stop.

Michael wanted *her*.

Betsy Warren says her horoscope describes her as a shy, homebody Cancer, while her color analysis chart proclaims her a classic Winter. She describes herself as a hopeful romantic. Betsy is single and works as a news and entertainment reporter for an American national cable television network. She traces her interest in writing to an early tendency to ask "what if?" and rewrite unhappy endings in her head. Her greatest ambition as a romance writer is to give readers the fun and pleasure of a truly happy ending.

Song
without Words

Betsy Warren

Harlequin Books

TORONTO • NEW YORK • LONDON
AMSTERDAM • PARIS • SYDNEY • HAMBURG
STOCKHOLM • ATHENS • TOKYO • MILAN

Original hardcover edition published in 1985
by Mills & Boon Limited

ISBN 0-373-02770-2

Harlequin Romance first edition June 1986

CHAPTER ONE

WITH a quiet sigh of satisfaction, Shauna Whitney sat back to contemplate the lines she had just finished typing. She scanned the words first with a copy editor's eye, searching for errors. Finding none, she re-read the lines for content, allowing herself a small smile of pride as she savoured the fruits of her creativity.

In an automatic gesture, she reached up and used the index finger of her right hand to push her large, horn-rimmed glasses back into place on the bridge of her nose. She nibbled at the soft pink curve of her lower lip as she continued to consider her writing. It wasn't absolutely right yet, but it definitely was one of her better efforts. And there was no disputing the fact that the crisp copy produced by the ultra-modern IBM Selectric at her office was far more professional to look at than the erratic lettering that stuttered out of her ancient Smith-Corona portable in her small apartment.

'Oh, Shauna. I thought I heard an after hours typewriter.'

The cultivated male voice broke in on her reverie. Starting slightly, Shauna looked up from her work and into the distinguished face of the head of her company's legal department.

'Oh, Mr Barkley. I—I didn't realise you were still here,' she said in her soft, well-modulated voice. A lady never raised her voice. That was one of the many tenets of 'proper' behaviour drilled into her from childhood by her strict and unrelenting Aunt Margaret. Unfortunately, her aunt's notions of 'proper' behaviour would not have been out of place in the Victorian era.

In recent months, Shauna had been trying—tentatively—to break out of the mould her aunt had established for her. Coming to New York City had been an act of defiance in many ways. Shauna sometimes wryly told herself that, at the age of twenty-two, she was finally going through an adolescent rebellion.

But a decade of living with Margaret Whitney had left its mark. Even though her aunt had been dead nearly nine months, Shauna could still sometimes hear her cool, precise voice chiding her. It was so difficult to escape the strictures of her upbringing. And Shauna was sensitive enough to know that, because of that upbringing, most people considered her quaintly old-fashioned . . . and some simply thought she was a strait-laced prude.

'I hope I wasn't disturbing you, sir,' she said hesitantly.

Mr Barkley waved the suggestion away. 'Not at all, not at all.' There were moments when Shauna thought Emmett Barkley was almost as out-of-place in New York City as she was. In his middle fifties, Barkley was the chief legal adviser for Sebastian Entertainment Enterprises, a music industry conglomerate headed by a man young enough to be his son. A Boston Brahmin by birth, Emmett Barkley conducted himself with a calm and courtly dignity that seemed better suited to the antique-furnished offices of some old-line law firm than to the flashy, often volatile world of show business.

'Is there something I can do for you, Mr Barkley?' Shauna enquired. She'd joined the secretarial staff of Sebastian Entertainment Enterprises' legal department six months before. In that time, she'd had only passing contact with Emmett Barkley.

'Yes, as a matter of fact there is. But, first, I do hope you're not here late on a Friday because of that copyright report. I know you're very conscientious, my dear, but that kind of devotion to duty—'

Shauna shook her head and smiled, her finely modelled features softening. 'No, it's some personal typing.' A line of concern creased her high, smooth brow. 'I—I hope you don't object to my using the office machine.'

'Good heavens, no.' He shook his head, then regarded her with approval, taking in her neat appearance and her poised but somewhat shy manner. 'Consider it a small perk for a job very well done.'

'Thank you.' The compliment brought a faint stain of pink up into her cheeks. She worked very hard, and it was satisfying to know that her efforts were being recognised. 'Now, you said there was something I could do for you?' She looked at him calmly, her wide, hazel eyes questioning from behind the protection of her glasses.

'If you would.' He held up a large manila envelope. 'These are the papers on that new British group Sebastian Enterprises has signed. Mr Sebastian wanted to check them over the weekend. Normally, I'd drop them off with him myself, but my wife and I have an engagement—'

'I'd be glad to take them upstairs, Mr Barkley,' she offered immediately.

'That's the problem. He's not in the building. He's downtown at a studio, supervising a recording session. At least that's where he was at last report.' He lifted a silvered brow significantly. Michael Sebastian—the owner and driving force behind Sebastian Entertainment Enterprises—was deservedly known as a man on the go. Like most executives in the business, he was 'bi-coastal'—that is, he shuttled back and forth between Los Angeles on the west coast and New York City on the east with exhausting regularity. He was also expanding his interests into Europe and the Far East.

'I'm rather concerned that if I send these papers to the studio by courier and he's not there, they'll be lost in transit,' Mr Barkley continued. 'So—'

'So you'd like me to track down Mr Sebastian and deliver the contracts for you?' she anticipated. 'I'd be very happy to.' She extended her hand to accept the envelope.

'Excellent. I do appreciate it. Here's the address of the studio.' He gave her a slip of paper. 'I'll call ahead to tell the security guard to expect you. They have to be very particular about allowing people in. Female fans

are always trying to burst in to see their favourite stars.'
He shook his head in mild disbelief.

Shauna glanced down at her trim tweed suit with a
trace of self-mockery. 'Somehow, I don't think anyone
will mistake me for a groupie,' she said lightly.

He chuckled. 'Oh, my, I should think not,' he
affirmed. 'Now, be certain to get receipts for the taxis.
And take a late meal on the company.'

'That's not necessary—'

'Yes, it is,' he said firmly. 'I insist.' He checked his
watch. 'I must be going. Thank you, Shauna. Have a
pleasant weekend.'

'The same to you, Mr Barkley.'

It took her a few minutes to restore her desk to its
usual pristine order. A place for everything and everything in its place. That was another one of her aunt's
rules. Margaret Whitney's standards of neatness had
been impossibly high for an eleven-year-old child, but
they'd instilled in Shauna an unshakeable desire to keep
things organised.

Carefully, she put the papers she had been typing into
a manila envelope and placed it—along with the envelope holding the papers for Michael Sebastian—into
her brown shoulder bag. Then she donned her camel-
coloured wrap coat, knotting the belt securely around
her slender waist, and exchanged her low-heeled pumps
for brown leather boots. She made a quick check to be
certain that she hadn't forgotten anything and made her
exit.

After signing out at the security desk in the lobby,
she went outside, shivering slightly against the brisk
October night air. Spotting an empty taxi cruising down
the street, she raised her arm in a decisive signal.

'Where to, lady?' the cabbie asked laconically, giving
her a quick glance in his rear view mirror as she slid into
the back seat.

Checking the slip of paper that Mr Barkley had given
her, Shauna read off the address.

'Oh, yeah, sure. I know where that is,' the driver

nodded, throwing the meter as he pulled out into traffic. 'They do recording gigs there, right?' He was fairly young with longish hair and a crooked grin. 'You in the music business?'

'Not exactly,' Shauna said politely. 'I work for Sebastian Entertainment—'

'SEE?' The driver was genuinely interested now. 'I should've guessed with you standing in front of their building. Hey, it's a good label—good names, good sound. And I've read a lot about your boss, Michael Sebastian. Man, he leads quite a life.' He sounded both approving and envious. 'And talented, too. He wrote that new single of Carla Decker's, didn't he? "Night Flight".' He sang a couple of bars, slightly off-key. 'You know, though, I've got to admit, Carla Decker could sing the phone book and I wouldn't mind listening. You know what I mean?'

'Umm . . .' Shauna made a neutral sound, although she knew precisely what the cabbie meant. Carla Decker —the 'Divine Decker' as she was referred to, both seriously and sardonically—was currently one of the hottest female vocalists on the pop scene. She was also, according to gossip, Michael Sebastian's latest lover.

'He must be something to work with.'

'I—I beg your pardon?'

'Michael Sebastian.'

'Oh.' In unthinking response to the feel of her glasses starting to slip down the bridge of her nose, Shauna pushed them back into place. 'Well, I don't actually work with him. Just for his company. I've only seen the man in the flesh once, to tell the truth.' She did not add that that once had been quite sufficient to allow her to decide that all the worst stories she'd heard about Michael Sebastian were probably true.

'I guess that's how it is in big business. Uh, will it bother you if I turn on some music?'

'No, that's all right.' She braced herself for a blast of rock-and-roll. Insted, the driver flipped his radio on to a station that played classical music, and she was treated to the final movement of a vaguely familiar piano concerto.

The charm of the melody soothed her, and she felt the tensions of a busy working week begin to ease away; however, she did not slump down in the seat. Correct posture was another one of Aunt Margaret's legacies. Although Shauna had been a self-conscious and very slender five-foot-six by her fifteenth birthday, she'd decided that being teased for her height at school was better than being scolded about slouching at home, so she'd developed an erect and graceful bearing in her teenage years.

'This is it,' the driver announced, pulling up in front of the address Shauna had given him. He read off the fare shown on the meter.

Shauna paid him promptly, adding a generous tip. Too much, Aunt Margaret probably would have said, but the driver had been very pleasant.

'Thanks,' he said, grinning as he gave her the necessary change.

'May I have a receipt?' she asked, remembering Emmett Barkley's admonition.

'Sure thing.' The cabbie reached for his receipt pad and scrawled down the pertinent information. 'Would you like me to wait around for you?' he enquired helpfully. 'You might have some trouble getting a cab in this neighbourhood.'

Shauna hesitated, considering the validity of his observation. The studio building was not located in the best part of the city.

'No—no, thank you,' she decided after a moment. 'I'm not certain how long my errand will take. But I appreciate your offering.'

'No problem. Have a good night.'

As Mr Barkley had promised, the security guard had been alerted to expect her.

'Mr Sebastian's still here?' Shauna verified.

'Yes, ma'am.' The guard nodded as she signed her name to his log in neat script. 'They're all here. Been

here for hours except for a meal break. Union require-
ment.' He shrugged. 'You know how that is.'

Shauna did. Working at SEE, she'd typed up plenty of
documents involving the stringent regulations governing
the use of union musicians and technicians. 'You said
Studio C?' she asked.

'That's the one. Third floor. Go left when you come
off the elevator, then all the way down the hall. You
can't miss it. Don't let the blinking light bother you. Just
be sure you go in the door marked "Control".'

'Thank you.'

Riding up in the lift, Shauna patted her chestnut-
brown hair several times to make certain her chignon
was still neat and securely pinned at the nape of her
neck. This was going to be a quick, easy errand. She'd be
in and out in a matter of minutes. Afterwards, she'd
have the guard downstairs call a radio cab for her.

The heels of her boots clicked a businesslike rhythm
on the linoleum of the hall floor as she followed the
instructions she'd been given. It wasn't a very glamorous
place: the corridors were a dingy grey and had an almost
institutional air.

Despite the guard's comment about the blinking light,
Shauna found herself momentarily intimidated by the
flashing red sign that read 'RECORDING! KEEP
OUT!' in no uncertain terms.

Squaring her shoulders and taking a deep breath, she
dismissed her anxiety and pushed open the heavy door
marked 'Control'. She entered as quietly as she could.

She could have charged in like the Seventh Cavalry for
all the difference it would have made, considering the
pandemonium going on inside.

Two intense-looking, blue-jeaned technicians were
huddling over a sound board, fiddling with levels while
they argued with mounting vigour over the quality of the
mix they were getting. A third technician was playing
back a synthesised audio track for a skinny, long-haired
young man who was registering his displeasure with
what he was hearing in a nasal voice. Another man,

dressed in a custom-tailored Italian suit, was on the phone, trying to conduct a call.

To add to the confusion, the intercom link between the control room and the studio was open, piping in a haphazard mix of expert but pointless drumming, keyboard noodling, and chord progressions from a pair of electric guitars.

Shauna winced at the cacophony, instinctively withdrawing into the corner by the door as she tried to sort out the chaos. She didn't see Michael Sebastian anywhere and, even if she had, it didn't take any great degree of perceptivity to figure out that she had walked into something that shouldn't be interrupted. She decided to bide her time for a bit.

Just as it appeared the confusion was about to hit its peak—or perhaps erupt into something worse—the door leading into the control room from the hall swung open, practically squashing Shauna back against the wall. Only quick reflex action kept her glasses from going flying.

The man responsible for the explosive entrance was none other than Michael Sebastian, and if he was aware that he'd come perilously close to causing serious bodily harm to someone, he gave no sign of it. A younger man followed in his dynamic wake, and he *did* notice something out of the ordinary. He gave Shauna a quick, puzzled look, but didn't say anything.

'Quiet!'

The two syllables ripped through the noise like a razor-edged sword, cutting off the racket almost instantaneously. The only person who ignored the command was the fashionably dressed man on the phone. Michael Sebastian dealt with that by the brutally simple expedient of taking the receiver away from the man and dropping it wordlessly back into its cradle.

'Hey, you just hung up on LA—' the man began to protest.

'Roger, I don't care if that was the moon,' Michael told him flatly. 'I said "quiet" and that's what I meant. If you want to make business calls during one of my recording sessions, do not—I repeat, do not—use my control room to do it. Go someplace else. Find a phone booth. And use your own dime while you're at it.'

The words came out like icy bullets, shooting down all possible dissent. Shauna was suddenly very thankful that Michael Sebastian had his back to her. She pressed herself against the wall, hoping to remain unobtrusive until things settled down. She got another curious look from the younger man who'd come in with Michael. He still did nothing to reveal her presence.

'Am I getting through to you, Roger?'

'Sure, Michael. Sorry,' the other man replied. He seemed to have developed a sudden fascination with the tips of his shoes.

'Thank you. Now—' Michael riveted everyone's attention. There was no question of who was in command. And the impact of his authority wasn't limited to the cramped, cluttered control room. The musicians had stopped playing around and were standing quietly. They could hear what was going on through the elaborate intercom system and see what was happening through the glass wall that divided the control room from the actual studio.

'Now—' Michael Sebastian repeated, playing the situation like a skilled musician. 'My brother and I have negotiated a small agreement. He will sing the number as written. I will refrain from strangling him and bringing in a new lead singer for Tempest.' He glanced at the young man who had come in with him. 'Right, Jamie?'

Jamie came to attention and snapped off a salute. 'Aye, aye, Captain,' he said precisely. There was a mixture of affectionate mockery and respect in the gesture. With a grin and yet another look at Shauna, he then turned and marched out through the connecting door and into the studio.

Jamie—of course! Everything clicked into place for Shauna. Jamie was Jamie Cord, Michael Sebastian's half-brother and lead singer for Tempest, one of the

fastest rising bands SEE had under contract. Tempest
had had two top-selling albums and a series of hit singles.
After several years of seasoning with limited club dates,
they'd done one tour as the opening act for a big name,
well-established band. They were now about to kick off
their own national tour. Shauna had heard another
Tempest album was in the works as well. Obviously, this
recording session was being devoted to the production
of that album. She wondered how much of Michael
Sebastian's presence in the studio was due to business
and how much was dictated by brotherly interest.

Whatever his motives, it was clear he knew exactly
what he wanted and wasn't about to settle for anything
less than perfection. He instructed the sound engineers
in detail, his command of their complex and often
obscure technical jargon serving as vivid proof of his
professional expertise.

From her refuge in the corner, Shauna studied him
with uneasy fascination. She could understand why most
of the women around SEE found him so devastatingly
attractive. His tall, leanly muscled body exuded a barely
leashed virility that had nothing to do with show business
posturing or phoney machismo. Michael Sebastian had a
bred-in-the-bone masculinity; he was the type of man
who would have no doubts about what he wanted and
no qualms about taking it. He also, to judge by his
phenomenal success in his first thirty-four years on
earth, was capable of holding what was his against all-
comers.

His profile was strong and uncompromising, unsoft-
ened by his thick and somewhat unruly thatch of dark
brown hair. His cheekbones were high and defiantly
moulded, his jaw strong and distinctly stubborn. His
nose had a faint crookedness to it, as though it had been
broken . . . in a fight, perhaps.

The thought of Michael Sebastian in a physical battle
sent a peculiar shiver down Shauna's spine. She recalled
the clichéd punch line: 'If you think *I* look bad, you
should see the *other* guy.'

While the rest of Michael's tanned face spoke of power and determination, his mouth hinted at a streak of sensuality. It could be a cruel mouth, Shauna mused, but it would be caressing, too—

She derailed this train of thought with a pang of mortification, feeling a hot rush of blood flood up into her face. She stiffened her body resolutely, a trifle shocked at the wayward direction her reflections had taken. Shauna had done her share of romantic daydreaming, but she'd never gone off into a semi-erotic fantasy about a flesh and blood man while standing in the same room with him!

It must be the atmosphere in here, she told herself. She certainly hadn't reacted to Michael Sebastian this way the other time she'd seen him! That little episode had left her with a very unfavourable impression of him—to say nothing of his tactics for dealing with women!

Shauna bit her lip in an unconsciously nervous gesture. She wanted to get out of the control room and away from the confusion. She glanced around anxiously, briefly considering making her presence known. She discarded the notion quickly.

Patience, Shauna, she counselled silently, recalling Aunt Margaret's many admonitions against impetuosity. After all, she told herself, this can't go on for *too* long.

Or perhaps it could.

Shauna had never been to a recording session before, but she'd heard horror stories from other SEE employees: stories about recording sessions that had dragged on for days, weeks—even months. Of course, none of those sessions had ever directly involved Michael Sebastian, but there was always a first time.

Shifting her weight slightly, and hugging her shoulder bag against her protectively, Shauna put that distressing scenario out of her mind. It didn't do to borrow trouble.

Michael was still talking with the engineers, sorting out one of the debates that had been going on when he'd made his abrupt entrance. Like the technicians, he was casually dressed. Yet he wore his tight-fitting black cord jeans and black turtle-neck sweater with an offhand elegance that set him apart. His clothing was impeccably functional and expensive.

Shauna tried not to think about the passing of time. She also tried to ignore the fact that she was becoming uncomfortably warm. She fought down the urge to remove her coat. The movement might attract unwanted attention.

To distract herself, Shauna stared through the glass panel into the studio, mentally reviewing what she knew about Tempest. With their major tour about to begin, the band had been getting a fair amount of press attention in recent days.

The drummer, Sam Gleason, was the son of a famous musician. Like everybody else in the group, he was in his mid-twenties and had been playing with bands since he was in his early teens. Slumped behind his drum set, he was beating an intricate, silent tattoo in the air.

The two guitarists were brothers—Henry and Franklin Stiles, inevitably nicknamed Hank and Frank because they looked enough alike to be twins. They were of medium height, lanky build, with close-cropped sandy brown hair. Each handled his guitar with loving expertise.

The keyboard player was Thaddeus 'Griz' Grizzard. He reminded Shauna of an overstuffed teddy bear. An untamed confusion of brown frizz exploded on his skull and his stocky body was encased in a fuzzy sweatsuit. He radiated an aura of good cheer and manic energy.

Finally, she turned her attention to Jamie Cord. He was pacing restlessly, mouthing words to himself.

Physically, he was shorter than his six-foot tall brother and of a slighter build. He was boyishly good-looking, with wavy brown hair and wide, long-lashed brown eyes. While he didn't possess Michael Sebastian's high-voltage sexual impact, he had an appealingly confident air spiced with a kind of free-spirited charm.

'OK,' Michael Sebastian's velvet dark voice interrupted her thoughts. He'd despatched the engineers back into position and taken a seat at the main mixing and control board. Running a hand through his dark and already tousled hair, he leaned forward and spoke into the intercom. 'All right, you musical madmen. We have been at this one cut for the entire session.'

'I thought it was beginning to sound repetitious,' Griz volunteered from his keyboard.

'It sounds even worse than that,' Michael shot back evenly, a hint of humour quirking his mouth. 'Now, as much as I would love to spend the night with you lunatics, I do have other things to do.'

'I thought Carla was in LA!' Jamie leered mockingly.

'She is in LA, baby brother.'

'And you still have something to do tonight? We all heard she'd signed you to an exclusive services contract.'

'You've got your facts backwards, Jamie,' his half-brother informed him. Michael remained silent as there was a knowing chorus of 'oh-hos' from the band.

As distasteful as Shauna found the barely veiled sexual innuendo—and as little as she wanted to hear the details of Michael Sebastian's relationship with Carla Decker—she did not fail to notice how skilfully the ribald bantering had been used to restore equilibrium in the studio. It reminded her of a shrewd and authoritative teacher allowing a wayward group of students to blow off some steam before bringing them back under control.

'If you're quite finished?' Michael enquired drily. The band members subsided obediently. 'Now, you know as well as I do where the problems are in this.' His voice had become businesslike but not indifferent. Michael Sebastian clearly cared about this particular song. His next words confirmed his creative stake in it. 'When I wrote this, I knew it was a departure from what you'd done before, but Tempest isn't going to have staying power unless you grow and take some chances. I'm going to have RJ play back part of the last take we did.

Listen up.' He glanced at the skinny engineer by the main reel-to-reel recording machines. 'RJ, pick it up at the beginning of the instrumental bridge.'

'Sure, Michael.' After a moment, the machine went into action and sound began pouring from the speakers in the control room. In what appeared to be an automatic response, the two technicians manning the mixing board began tinkering with their complicated gear, delicately regulating levels and checking various readings.

The instrumental bridge was a hauntingly provocative interplay of guitar and keyboard spiced with a strong beat from Sam Gleason's drums. It *was* a departure from Tempest's previous work—a sophisticated adaption of their basically straightforward rock sound.

Jamie's voice—a strong tenor with an attractive huskiness to it—joined in the mix.

> Nothing lasts forever.
> Not even when it seems this right.
> What we're feeling may be gone in the morning—
> But it's all that's important tonight.

The lyrics continued in the same vein through the verse and the chorus, the music picking up a throbbing intensity. It had a compelling quality to it . . . but there was something missing.

Shauna closed her eyes for a moment, just concentrating on the words. They'd been written by a man who had few, if any, romantic illusions about life. He dealt with sexuality directly, expressing his desires frankly. He did not make promises in order to get those desires fulfilled.

Jamie's delivery of the lyrics didn't quite provide the knowing edge the song needed. It was probably the difference in age and experience between him and his half-brother, Shauna reflected. While Jamie Cord was in his mid-twenties and a rising star, he was still something of an untempered boy. Michael Sebastian was very emphatically a man.

'Cut it, RJ,' Michael ordered abruptly. The engineer

punched a button and killed the sound. 'Any comments?'

'I still think the bass line is ragged,' Frank said, looking down at his guitar as though accusing it of a major crime.

'Yeah, something about the instrumental is still a bit off,' Sam contributed from behind his drum set.

Jamie shook his head vehemently. 'No. Come on, guys. The problem is the vocal track.' He jammed his hands into the back pockets of his jeans, frowning. 'It's not hot enough. I want to get the girl into bed, right? But I'm not supposed to be singing her to sleep!'

'Hey, it's not that bad,' Hank declared. The other members of Tempest chimed in supportively.

'What we need is women,' Griz said. He outlined the shape of a well-endowed female body. 'Something to get the old juices flowing again.'

'The way you five reportedly have had the "old juices" flowing the last couple of weeks may be part of the problem,' Michael informed him sardonically.

'Griz has a point, though,' Jamie said. 'It's hard to get energised for this kind of song when we have to do it over and over again in a room full of guys.' The other band members nodded in sympathy. 'Much as we're one big happy family, an all-male recording session is not what turns us on.'

'Oh, I don't know about that,' the drummer drawled. 'When the light hits old Griz's hair just right, he looks kind of cute.'

Michael's profile tightened, a look of impatience passing over his face. The long and powerful fingers of his right hand—musician's fingers, Shauna thought fleetingly—tapped on the control panel.

'Shall I call Dial-a-Date?' he enquired sarcastically.

'Michael—' The well-dressed man identified as Roger leaned forward helpfully. 'I could get a couple of—'

Michael shook his head decisively. 'No, Roger. I know the well-prepared manager comes equipped with a little black book filled with the names and numbers of lots of willing and eager young things, but I don't want any groupies cluttering up this recording session. Thank you.'

'We need inspiration, Michael,' Jamie declared, spreading his hands.

'Close your eyes and fantasise,' Michael recommended coolly.

'Well—' Jamie's eyes narrowed. 'How about the fox in the control room? Or do you have her signed to an exclusive services contract as a door stop or something?'

It took Shauna a moment to realise, with a horrible sinking feeling in the pit of her stomach, that the 'fox' Jamie had so suggestively mentioned was her. During that awful moment, every eye in the place swung in her direction, darted speculatively towards Michael Sebastian, then back to her.

Michael Sebastian turned, surprise and irritation etched plainly on his strong features. As he focused on Shauna, however, his expression altered radically. The change only lasted for a second or so before he got himself back under control, but for the space of time he let whatever he was feeling show, he looked like a man who had been dealt a sudden and very telling emotional blow.

He rose from his seat in a lithe movement and seemed to loom over her—tall, dark, and distinctly dangerous.

'What the hell are you doing here?' he demanded in an icy voice.

CHAPTER TWO

NEARLY every article written about Michael Sebastian mentioned his eyes. Framed by dark, thick lashes, they were an arresting jade green flecked with glints of gold and deep blue. If not precisely windows into his soul, they at least gave some hint of his mood at any particular moment.

Shauna felt pinned to the wall by emerald lasers. She could hear her heart pounding. The room had grown so quiet that she suspected everyone else could hear it, too.

'Well?' he asked.

She took a deep breath. She had a perfectly reasonable explanation for her presence in the control room. There was no need for her to be so nervous—or for him to stare at her in such an accusatory manner.

'I—I'm Shauna Whitney, Mr Sebastian,' she replied at last, amazed that the words came out so steadily.

'How did you get in here?' His eyes had narrowed slightly, and she had the fleeting impression that he had recognised her somehow. But that was ridiculous—

She cleared her throat. 'The guard downstairs—'

'The guard downstairs is paid to keep people from getting in here, not to roll out the red carpet.'

'But—' she started to open her shoulder bag. 'I have something for you—'

'I can imagine what,' he retorted rudely. His eyes ran over her assessingly. 'Are you dressed underneath that coat?' he enquired outrageously.

'Wha—?' Her voice jumped an octave. 'I beg your pardon!'

'The last enterprising female who barged into one of my recording sessions had on a raincoat and Chanel Number Five. Period.'

For a moment, shock left Shauna absolutely speech-less. She had the distinct feeling Michael Sebastian didn't find the memory of that particular young woman altogether irritating. She drew herself up proudly, bit-terly aware that his height advantage forced her to look up at him in order to make eye contact.

'Mr Sebastian,' she said stiffly, 'if you'll allow me to explain—'

He shook his head decisively, bulldozing over her words. 'No explanations. Tempest wants inspiration. You're not much, sweetheart, but you're the best we can do on short notice. Come with me.'

'Coming with' Michael Sebastian consisted of being grabbed by the arm and forcibly escorted out of the control room and into the studio.

She could feel the bruising grip of his fingers clear through the thick woollen material of her coat sleeve. For one furious moment, she considered slamming him with her shoulder bag. A quick look from those vivid green eyes—eyes that seemed to say he'd sensed her violent impulse—warned her about the foolishness of such a move.

'Frank, get the lady a stool,' Michael ordered calmly.

'Do you mind?' Shauna hissed, glaring at him.

'Yes, I do,' he snapped. 'Take off your coat.'

'Mr Sebastian—'

'Off!' He still had his hand on her upper arm.

He's insane, Shauna thought. He's also the most ill-mannered, overbearing brute—

'Um, let me help you,' Frank said politely after he'd produced the stool as instructed. He seemed slightly bewildered by what was transpiring, but far from hostile.

'Thank you,' Shauna said automatically, then shot her captor an acid look. 'If Mr Sebastian would let go of me for one moment—'

He released her so abruptly that she nearly staggered. Wasn't anyone going to do anything? Were they all going to stand around there, watching her?

'We're waiting, Shauna,' Michael informed her.

Apparently, they were.

'It's Miss Whitney, Mr Sebastian,' she gritted out frigidly. With all the dignity she could muster, she put down her bag, undid the tie belt of her coat, then slipped the garment off. Michael took the coat and handed it to Frank who draped it neatly over another stool then returned wordlessly to his guitar.

Again, the disconcerting green eyes ran over her. She had the appalling sensation the owner of those eyes knew precisely what kind of underwear she had on and that he found the modest nylon and lace lingerie laughably chaste. The women he knew probably wore sheer wisps of satin—or nothing at all.

'Well, you certainly are dressed, Miss Whitney,' he observed mockingly, taking in the tailored tweed suit and demure ivory silk blouse. 'Sit down.' He more or less deposited her on the stool Frank had brought over for her.

The jolt of being seated jarred her glasses and she reached up to push them back into place.

'No.' Michael forestalled her by brushing her hand aside and removing the glasses completely. The touch of his fingers went through her like an electric shock.

Shauna blinked indignantly, feeling remarkably vulnerable. Her vision wasn't that bad, actually—an ordinary case of short-sightedness—but she was used to the protective shield of her glasses. 'Will you please give me back—'

'Later.' Michael surveyed her silently as though inspecting a puzzle of some kind. Before she realised his intention, he'd reached around to the back of her head with both hands and thrust his fingers unceremoniously into her glossy chignon, jerking loose most of the pins that were holding it in place. 'Hold still,' he advised her as she twisted away, 'This isn't going to hurt.'

'Stop it!' She could feel her heavy chestnut hair tumbling over her shoulders as he raked his fingers down through the auburn-highlighted tresses like a comb. 'Ouch!'

'I told you to hold still,' he reminded her as he finally stopped playing with her hair. For a moment, he kept her head cradled between his hands, his long fingers touching at the back of her skull while his thumbs ran gently, teasingly, around the sensitive outer rims of her ears.

'Do you mind?' she asked tautly, feeling a shiver go through her as he withdrew his hands, his fingers stroking lingeringly across the slender line of her throat. She swallowed hard, forcing herself to look him straight in the eye.

'Not at all,' he replied with a hateful degree of self-possession. There was a mixture of amusement, interest, and something else she couldn't quite interpret, in his expression as he studied her intently once again. 'That's a big improvement. You seem to be inspiration material after all. Especially with your hair down.' A slight edge in his voice gave an unmistakable double meaning to the words. Shauna felt herself flushing with anger and embarrassment, but before she could voice her feelings, Michael had turned smoothly to Jamie. He'd been watching the confrontation with unabashed fascination.

'OK, little brother,' Michael said drily. 'The "fox" in the control room. Shauna Whitney, Jamie Cord. Jamie Cord, Shauna Whitney.' He performed the introductions in a manner that turned the elementary courtesy into something close to an insult. 'You've got about two minutes to get to know each other.'

If she'd been thinking clearly, Shauna would have simply got up at that point and stalked out of the studio. Two things stopped her from doing this. First, she was not thinking very clearly. Second, she knew instinctively that Michael Sebastian would have no compunction about dragging her back—probably by the hair—if she did try to leave before he was finished with her. She watched him walk back into the control room with an easy, jungle-cat stride.

Jamie cleared his throat, drawing her attention. 'So —uh—Shauna—do you come here often?'

The enquiry was so patently inappropriate that she could only stare at him blankly, wondering if he, too, was crazy. Or perhaps *she* was the one who had gone mad.

He gave her a reassuring grin. 'Michael did tell us to get to know each other,' he pointed out with a wink, plainly signalling that he was on her side.

Shauna was not quite ready to respond to the sympathetic overture—particularly when it came from the person whose offhand remark had landed her in this humiliating predicament. She reached up and brushed her hair back behind her ears. Her hands were trembling.

'I suppose you always do what he tells you to?' she retorted.

'He *is* my boss.'

To her horror, Shauna gave a semi-hysterical giggle. 'H-he's my boss, too, actually,' she got out.

'You work for Michael—SEE?' Jamie asked, visibly astonished. Given the way his half-brother had treated her—and her own manner, for that matter—Shauna couldn't blame him for being so surprised.

She nodded once. 'I work for Sebastian Entertainment Enterprises. At least I did before this evening.' She sighed. 'I came here to deliver some papers from the legal department—'

Jamie gave a long whistle. 'Oh, man, why didn't you say something?'

Shauna glared briefly in the direction of the control room. She could see Michael conferring with two technicians, gesturing commandingly. 'Because a certain individual wouldn't let me get a word in edgeways,' she replied tartly.

'Yeah, he does tend to get a little overpowering at times,' Jamie conceded. 'Look, Shauna, I'm really sorry I got you into this mess. I was just joking around. If you'll help us get this track right, I'll help you get everything straightened out.'

'We'll all help you get everything straightened out,'

Griz interpolated, giving her a thumbs up signal. Shauna realised that the other members of Tempest had been eavesdropping on her conversation with Jamie. She flushed a bit and glanced around at them, comforted by the fact that they were regarding her with various degrees of friendly interest.

'What am I supposed to do?' she asked.

'You don't have to do anything,' Jamie assured her quickly. 'Just sit there and look terrific. Hey, Hank—' he spoke over his shoulder, 'give me the extra headset, will you, please?'

'Sure, Jamie.'

'Okay, thanks.' Jamie accepted the black and grey headset from the guitarist. He placed one of the padded earphones against Shauna's ear. 'Hold it,' he instructed. 'That way, you'll be able to get the full effect. We've already got the main instrumental tracks laid down. What we're going for now is the vocal.'

Shauna nodded her comprehension. She warmed to the friendly understanding in Jamie's dark eyes. He was very different from his half-brother.

'Do you suppose we can get started?' Michael's voice drawled through the intercom.

She stiffened, tension flooding back into her body. Jamie gave her an encouraging grin as though telling her that the ordeal would soon be over. He slipped on his own headset.

'Okay, Michael,' he announced, giving the earphones a small adjustment. 'Let's go for a gold record.'

'Let's go for platinum,' Sam Nelson amended.

'Let's get done and go for dinner,' Griz suggested with amiable practicality.

'Amen to that,' Michael returned with a hint of humour.

There was a brief silence during which Shauna saw the band members exchange looks, plainly willing that this take work. Jamie closed his eyes, concentrating on what he had to do. Uncertain of what was expected of her, Shauna simply remained where she was, poised on the

stool with the headphone pressed to her ear, still seeth-
ing with resentment at Michael Sebastian.

'We're rolling,' a technician's voice informed them.

The same musical bridge she had heard before flooded
into her ear. Jamie nodded, picking up the beat, his body
swaying slightly. Then, at just the right moment, he
began to sing.

This time, it worked. Perhaps Shauna's presence had
something to do with it—perhaps Michael Sebastian's
prodding was the reason—but, in either case, the lyrics
came out with a smooth, sensual energy. Jamie's phras-
ing supported and enriched the provocative poetry of
the words, blending flawlessly with the music. After the
first line, he opened his eyes and began to sing directly at
Shauna, performing for her with flattering and flirtatious
intensity.

Yet it was the song—not the singer—that moved her
in a disturbing and unfamiliar fashion. It was the thought
of the man who had written the words and music that
sent a shiver of anticipation down her spine. She had
always been keenly sensitive to the skilled use . . . and
the seductive power . . . of language.

The final chord faded. There was a moment of elo-
quent silence as the band members looked back and
forth at each other. Then a kind of giddy pandemonium
broke out.

'All right!' Jamie crowed triumphantly, yanking off
his headset and tossing it aside rather carelessly. 'If you
guys in the control room didn't like that, you can get
yourself another singer!' He caught Shauna impulsively
by the shoulders, pulling her off the stool, and gave her
an exuberantly affectionate kiss. Before she could ex-
tricate herself from his enthusiastic embrace, she
was surrounded by the other members of Tempest,
being bombarded by introductions, compliments and
congratulations.

A strong-fingered hand grasped Shauna, drawing her
out of Jamie's encircling arms and turning her around.
Catching her breath, she stared up into Michael

Sebastian's sensual, compelling face with a sense of
helplessness. Her heart was racing. His green gaze
moved over her delicate features in lingering scrutiny
before it came to rest on her slightly parted lips.

'I don't—' she began to protest. 'Please—'

He bent his head and kissed her, slowly and deliberately. His hard, demanding mouth closed expertly over
her soft lips in a caress that drove all rational thought out
of her mind for a moment. The tip of his tongue flicked
teasingly over her tender lower lip, sending a tremor
through her body.

The contact only lasted a few seconds, but it left her
quivering on the edge of responsiveness. Her hazel eyes
were wide and almost dazed. She was too caught up in
her own tumultuous reactions to notice the oddly regretful look that passed fleetingly over Michael's face.

'My, my, Miss Whitney,' he drawled as he released
her. 'You are a lady of very unexpected talents.'

Something about his mocking comment snapped her
control. She'd been cross-examined, ordered about,
manhandled, and publicly kissed by this infuriatingly
arrogant man. Now, he had the unmitigated gall to mock
her!

She slapped him, hitting him hard enough to leave the
reddened imprint of her slender fingers on his cheek.

He caught her wrist in what seemed to be a reflex
action, a dangerous light coming into his jade eyes. The
rest of the studio was frozen in shock.

'Oh!' Shauna made the sound involuntarily. Whether
it was in protest or apology, she didn't know. After so
many years of measuring her responses in accordance
with Aunt Margaret's standards—reining in her temper,
stifling an impish sense of humour—she had suddenly
surrendered to impulse. She had done exactly what she
felt like doing . . . but to her employer!

'Not exactly the way to impress the boss, Miss
Whitney,' Michael told her with a taunting smile. 'Even
if he won't let you get a word in edgeways.'

Hot blood rushed up into her face as she realised the

implication of his words. Her eyes darted in the direction of the control room then back to him.

'You—you knew!' she accused him with loathing in her voice. 'You h-heard what I said to Jamie over the intercom!'

He didn't deny it. Rather, he confirmed the truth of her charge with an ironic little nod.

'You knew and you still—You—you—' Shauna choked. Angry as she was, the inhibitions of her up-bringing still gripped her, preventing her from spitting out the epithets she was thinking. 'How dare you?' she demanded, jerking herself away from him, her breasts heaving as she glared at him. 'I think you are the most despicable man I've ever met, Mr Sebastian. I wouldn't work for you if you paid me!'

'I do pay you,' he pointed out.

She made an exasperated gesture, ignoring the voice inside her that was warning her she was about to do something she would regret.

'Not any more!' she shot back, stalking over to where she had deposited her shoulder bag. Shauna opened the tote, her fingers shaking with rage. Extracting the manila envelope inside, she flung it in his direction, not caring where it landed. 'That's why I "barged" in on your precious recording session, Mr Sebastian. It's from Mr Barkley. The papers you had to have for the weekend. Believe me, I wouldn't have come anywhere near you if it hadn't been for them!'

She snatched up her coat, her stormy gaze sweeping the studio. 'I'd wish you bad luck with the rest of the night, but I happen to think Tempest is a terrific band. Besides, they have enough bad luck. They have to work for you!' With that, she marched over to the studio door and yanked it open.

'Shauna—' Michael's voice was sharp.

She whirled back, her chestnut hair fanning out with a silken life of its own. 'Oh, don't bother to fire me,' she gritted out. 'I quit!'

Tossing her head in a defiant gesture, she walked out,

taking great satisfaction in slamming the door behind her with all the force she could muster.

The next two days constituted one of the worst weekends of her life. Shauna couldn't eat, she couldn't sleep, and her mind rebelliously kept replaying every detail of the disastrous scene in the studio. She found herself waiting for Michael Sebastian to appear at her apartment door demanding a grovelling apology . . . or worse.

The awful part of it was, she liked her work at SEE very much. It paid well, it was challenging, and it had given her a chance to prove she could make a life for herself without following the blueprint mapped out by her late aunt.

Shauna had been taken in by her aunt at the age of eleven after a New Year's Eve car accident left her an orphan. Margaret Whitney was in her late forties at the time, unmarried by choice, and not particularly fond of children. But she was Shauna's nearest living relative, and she knew where her duty lay.

An adoption dictated by duty—not affection—had been painful for a child of Shauna's loving and sometimes fanciful spirit. In an attempt to win her aunt's approval, she'd learned to curb her natural impulses and conform to the pattern of living Margaret Whitney deemed correct. She'd allowed herself to be bent . . . but not broken.

To please her aunt, she'd given up the idea of pursuing an English literature degree in college and taken a secretarial course instead. It was more practical, her aunt decreed.

Shauna had not truly realised the degree of resentment and rebellion growing within her until after Margaret Whitney's death of a sudden heart attack. Until the day she died, Shauna had tried, desperately, to please her aunt—to win her love. It was only when she was informed of her aunt's will—a coldly worded document that left nearly everything to her favoured charities

—that she knew how miserably she'd failed.

Shauna hadn't cared about the money. But it would have meant everything if the will had contained a small phrase of affection . . . a hint that Margaret Whitney had considered her niece something more than an obligation.

The will had offered one liberating piece of news. She now had access to a small trust fund left for her by her parents. Shauna had seized this as an inmate might seize the key to his prison. She'd taken the money and used it to finance her move to New York City . . . and to a new life, she hoped.

Now all her dreams and aspirations were in jeopardy. Perhaps her aunt had been right about the dangers of unbridled emotions after all.

Staring at her reflection in the bathroom mirror, Shauna blinked uncomfortably. On top of everything else, she'd left her glasses in the studio when she'd made her dramatic exit. Pride had made it impossible for her to go back and retrieve them.

Fortunately, she had a pair of contact lenses she'd purchased when she'd first come to New York. They'd been part of a tentative effort to 'change her image'. But she'd quickly discovered that altering her appearance didn't change the way she felt about life. It did, however, lead some people to expect a number of things she was not ready to give. She'd quickly retreated to her normal, restrained style. It was safer.

With a little shiver, Shauna recalled the touch of Michael Sebastian's fingers as he'd taken off her glasses and the definite flair of appreciation she'd seen in his eyes as he'd pulled her neatly pinned hair into disorder about her shoulders. It had been an unsettling experience, but there had been something disturbingly pleasurable in the sudden flash of attraction she'd felt spark between them.

Was she really so different with her glasses off and her hair down? Studying herself in the mirror, Shauna decided that the question sounded like something out of a corny old movie. Besides, no matter what she looked like on the outside, inside she was still a twenty-two-year-old woman who had experienced less of life than many sixteen- and seventeen-year-old girls!

Carefully, she shadowed her eyelids with a touch of green powder then coated her lashes with an extra layer of mascara. She added a quick brush of peach blusher to her cheeks and a gloss of colour to her lips. She had never noticed—although more than a few men had —that the full, sweet curve of her mouth was intriguingly at odds with her untouched and often distant air.

Straightening the suede tie belt of her heathery green wool dress, she decided it was time to go to face the inevitable.

'You may be headed for the unemployment line,' she told herself wryly, 'but you might as well make your final exit from Sebastian Entertainment Enterprises with dignity!'

Walking into the main room of her apartment, she picked up her brown leather shoulder bag only to groan in frustration as the contents of it spilled out on the floor.

The frustration changed into something much worse as the manila envelope she'd placed in the bag on Friday night opened too, freeing a sheaf of neatly typed legal papers.

For an awful moment, Shauna thought she might be physically sick. Kneeling down, she picked up the papers with trembling fingers, hoping she might be hallucinating, but knowing she wasn't.

She'd given Michael Sebastian the wrong envelope! In the midst of the confusion, goaded by anger, she'd kept the envelope containing the documents Mr Barkley had entrusted to her. Instead, she'd thrown *her* envelope at Michael!

The envelope containing her poetry.

Shauna had written poetry even as a young child. While she considered her talent modest, writing gave her great pleasure. It was also a safe outlet for her deepest feelings, tapping into a wellspring of emotion she was sometimes astonished to find within herself. This made her poetry intensely personal. It was a very private thing. The thought of having it read by Michael Sebastian made her feel terribly vulnerable.

She started violently as the phone rang. Picking it up, she murmured a distracted greeting into the receiver. She was still clutching the business papers in her hand, not wanting to believe that she had been responsible for such a mix-up.

'Shauna, is that you?'

She recognised the urbane tones of Emmett Barkley. 'M-Mr Barkley?' He undoubtedly was calling her to say her services were no longer required.

'I'm glad I caught you in. I've just had a conversation with Mr Sebastian about you—'

Shauna made an involuntary sound of distress.

'Shauna? I beg your pardon—'

She took a deep breath. Don't be such a coward, she told herself fiercely. You did this to yourself. Face up to it! 'Mr Barkley, I can explain—'

'There's no need for that,' he cut in smoothly. 'Michael's explained the whole thing. You made quite an impression on him Friday evening. Congratulations.'

Shauna shook her head, wondering if she was hearing things. She was bitterly aware of the kind of impression she must have made on Michael Sebastian. What she couldn't understand was why her boss—her *ex*-boss, she corrected herself ruefully—was discussing her actions in such an approving tone. 'I—I'm a little confused,' she said hesitantly.

'Michael—Mr Sebastian—would like to see you as soon as possible.'

Her stomach knotted. So that was it! For better or worse, she'd had the last word in their confrontation at the studio, and Michael Sebastian did not strike her as the kind of man who would let anybody walk away from him after having the last word. So, he wanted to even the score—or, more likely, settle the game completely in his favour. Well, she was just going to have to accept the consequences of what she'd done. She glanced at her watch.

'I can be into the office in about twenty minutes, Mr Barkley,' she said, calculating.

'No. No, that's the reason I called you. Michael isn't coming into the office today. He flew out to Los Angeles and back over the weekend and he's taking off for London in a few hours. He felt it would be pointless to come into the office for such a short time. So—'

'So, he wants me to come to his a-apartment?' Shauna guessed, shuddering at the kind of private scene Michael Sebastian probably had in store for her.

'Precisely. A bit unorthodox, I realise,' Mr Barkley commented drily, hearing the tension in her voice and evidently misinterpreting the cause of it. 'Still, in the years I've known him, I must say that Michael has never been particularly restrained by the dictates of orthodoxy. Now, this is his address—' He read off the location of an apartment building on the upper East Side. 'He's expecting you,' he added. 'And the doorman has your name.'

If Mr Sebastian's expecting me, I certainly wouldn't want to keep him waiting, Shauna thought mutinously, but she kept the resentment and uncertainty out of her voice as she said, 'Thank you, sir.'

She left her apartment a few minutes later and was fortunate enough to be able to hail a cab almost as soon as she stepped outside her building. She gave the driver the address and sat back, her hands nervously twisting the shoulder strap of her bag as she tried to control her mounting anxiety.

Michael Sebastian lived in an exclusive and obviously expensive co-op complex. Everything about the place spelled power, money, and good taste. After checking her name and business, a nattily dressed doorman waved her through a lobby that had the discreet elegance she associated with glossy decorating magazines. The quiet luxury of the place extended to the handsomely appointed lift that took her swiftly and silently up to the proper floor.

The door to Michael's apartment swung open just as she raised her hand to ring the bell. Michael stood there, radiating a virile magnetism that hit her like a blow.

They regarded each other silently for a long moment. His dark hair was ruffled, there was a certain heaviness to his eyelids, and he was wearing only a pair of faded jeans. He looked as though he'd just got out of bed.

Shauna discovered that her mouth had gone dry. The tip of her tongue darted out to moisten her lips. 'M-Mr Barkley said you wanted to see me,' she said finally, feeling at a hopeless disadvantage.

'I want to do more than see you,' he replied, pausing as he fought back a yawn. 'Sorry. It was a long night. Come in.'

'But, I—'

'In, Miss Whitney.' The lazy indolence disappeared.

Reluctantly, she obeyed, giving him a wary glance as he shut the door. The sheer physical impact of him made her nervous. His body was powerfully but leanly built, without an ounce of superfluous fat. She could see the smooth play of muscle beneath the tanned skin of his torso and arms. The tight fit of his well-worn jeans left little of the lower half of his very masculine physique to the imagination.

'You don't have to look like that,' he said with an unexpected, teasing grin. He helped her out of her coat.

'Like what?' she countered defensively.

'Like you're expecting me to pounce on you at any second. Have no fear. I make it a rule never to seduce my employees on Mondays.'

She stiffened. 'I'm not your employee,' she retorted unwisely, then winced, realising how the remark could be taken.

One dark brow quirked upward and his green eyes ran over her in blatant but mocking assessment. His gaze made her disconcertingly aware of her body and its delicate femininity. 'Is that a challenge or an invitation?' he enquired.

She took a deep breath, ruefully conceding that she had given him the opening for such a question. 'Neither,' she answered. 'It was a simple statement of fact.'

'You're talking about the fact that you quit SEE, I take it?' he enquired mildly. 'Yet, here you are, aren't you? Just because Emmett Barkley said I wanted to see you. Tell me, did you inform him you'd quit?'

'I—' She bit her lip. She had the distinct feeling she was being toyed with by an expert. It was not a feeling she liked. 'No. No, I didn't.'

'Smart girl. It'll save you the awkwardness of explaining that you've changed your mind.'

'That I've—Just what makes you think I've changed my mind?' she demanded, irritated by the arrogance she detected in his tone.

'You lost your temper Friday night—'

'I was provoked!'

'Granted.' He shrugged that aside as a matter of little or no consequence. 'Justified or not, you still blew your cool. And I learned a long, long time ago, a woman in a flaming temper will say a lot of things she doesn't really mean.' His sensual, well-cut mouth curved into a faintly cynical smile. 'Especially when she's making a big exit.'

'I don't say things I don't mean,' she informed him coolly. However much she might regret what had happened at the recording session, she had meant what she'd said to him.

'Then you're unique among your sex,' he drawled sardonically.

'Look—'

'I suppose you spent a serenely restful weekend contemplating the pleasant prospect of cleaning out your desk at SEE and hitting the pavement to look for a new job?'

For a moment, furious hazel eyes met amused green ones in silent conflict. He was far too perceptive.

'Well, Miss Whitney?'

'What do you want me to do, Mr Sebastian?' she snapped, drawing herself up. 'Drop down on to my knees and apologise? Beg for my job?'

'The first thing I want you to do is to stop calling me Mr Sebastian. My name is Michael. Use it. Because I intend to call you Shauna. The second thing I want you to do is to forget what happened Friday night. Forget that I was something less than my usual charming self to you and I'll forget that you pack a powerful right-hand wallop.' He gave her a slow, distinctly sexy smile as his jade eyes lingered briefly on her mouth. 'On second thought, maybe I'll keep the wallop in mind. It might help keep me in line.'

Shauna felt a disconcerting tug of attraction. She steeled herself against it with a sense of unease. She had no intention of being manoeuvred—or seduced—into a flirtation with a man who was out of her league in just about every category imaginable.

'Are you saying . . . I still have my job at SEE?' she asked cautiously, fighting an urge to edge away from him. It was one thing to be on her guard. It was another to let him know how badly off balance he made her feel.

'Unless you like the idea of being out of work better.'

'But—why?' she blurted out. The question held a mixture of hope, bewilderment, and suspicion.

'I have my reasons, believe me. Look, come in to the living room and I'll lay things out for you.'

Intrigued yet wary, Shauna followed him, taking in her surroundings with unwilling interest. The foyer of the apartment opened into a large, two-levelled room. The walls were an eggshell colour and the floors were dark polished wood. The upholstered furniture matched the walls and was of the modular, functional variety —designed to be rearranged as necessity or whim dictated. One wall was dominated by a built-in home entertainment centre which contained a television, video equipment, and an elaborate stereo system. Scores of albums, video cassettes, and audio tapes were neatly arranged on the shelves constructed around the equipment.

The stark, high-tech feel of the place was softened by the eclectic collection of artwork—paintings, prints and sculptures—displayed throughout the room. It was casually but thoughtfully arranged, not simply used for effect.

She was unaware of how eloquently the play of expression over her delicate features betrayed her appreciation and her surprise.

'Not exactly what you expected, Shauna?'

'I—' She met his curious gaze uncertainly. 'No—no, not really,' she went on honestly after a moment. 'I certainly didn't expect to find a grand piano here.'

A Steinway concert piano was positioned in one corner of the room. It was evident that its polished, classic elegance was not just for show. Two messy stacks of sheet music sat on the floor beside it along with a portable tape recorder. There were sheets of paper propped up on the rack over the keyboard as well.

'You had me pegged as the Moog synthesizer type?'

'Something like that,' she agreed. He gestured for her to sit down and she did so with unconscious grace. Without speaking, he picked up a moss green pullover that had been tossed over the back of a chair. He tugged it on over his head. The rich colour suited him perfectly and the snug fit of the knit emphasised the athletic lines of his upper body.

'Can I get you some coffee?' he asked suddenly, running a hand carelessly through his already disordered hair.

Shauna realised she was staring at him and dropped her eyes. 'No.' It came out more abruptly than she intended. 'No, thank you,' she amended.

He regarded her narrowly for a moment. 'I make you nervous, don't I?' It was really more of a statement than a question. 'I wonder why.'

Shauna studied her neatly trimmed nails. 'I'm not

nervous,' she contradicted. 'It's just that—I'm not used to doing business like this.'

'Like this?'

'In . . . in someone's apartment.' She wasn't used to doing *anything* in a man's apartment!

'Ah. I see.'

She glanced at him sharply, but his expression was unreadable. 'Besides . . . after what happened Friday—'

'I told you to forget that.'

'How can I? To begin with, you've got my—'

'Glasses?' She'd meant to say he had the wrong packet of papers. 'I know, I realised I still had them after you stormed out. They're perfectly safe.' He studied her appraisingly. 'I like you much better without them. It's criminal to hide yourself behind those things.'

'I don't hide behind my glasses,' she protested, aware of a perverse feeling of pleasure at his implied compliment. 'I need them to see.'

'You don't appear to be having any trouble with that.'

'I—I happen to be wearing contacts at the moment,' she admitted.

'In that case, I may keep your glasses for a bit longer. And if I can get you to let your hair down as well—'

Involuntarily, she raised one hand in a defensive gesture as though to save her chignon from a repeat of what had happened the previous Friday. 'Mr Sebastian—' she began angrily. He was outrageous!

'Michael,' he corrected calmly.

She lowered her hand slowly. 'Please—'

'I'm sure you can say it, Shauna,' he prompted, stressing her name with caressing deliberation. 'Two easy syllables. Michael.'

'Mr—Michael!' She knew she wasn't going to get anywhere if she didn't give in on this point. 'Michael,' she repeated firmly. 'What I was trying to say—to explain—is that I . . . I gave you the wrong envelope on Friday night.'

'So I noticed.' He sat down in the chair opposite her, stretching his long legs out.

Shauna's heart plummeted. Deep down, she had cherished the desperate hope that he might not have checked inside the envelope.

'I brought the papers Mr Barkley wanted you to have,' she said, opening her shoulder bag and extracting the proper manila envelope. She extended it to him. 'I'm very sorry about the confusion. I—I hope it didn't cause any problems.'

He accepted the envelope and tossed it offhandedly down beside him without checking the contents. 'No problem,' he said laconically.

She waited for a moment, her stomach knotting with tension. 'I—Do you have the envelope I gave you?' she asked finally, sounding anxious.

'I've got it, and you'll get it back in due time. First, I have a proposition for you—a business proposition.'

'Oh?' She struggled to keep her voice neutral.

'Yes, "oh". I need a secretary-assistant here in New York for two weeks. Starting next Monday.'

'But you already have a secretary!'

'True. Unfortunately—or fortunately, if you're a romantic—Dee has suddenly decided to get married. She's heading off on her honeymoon on Friday.' He gave a crooked grin. 'She's been in a pink haze for the past month.'

'But—'

'The girl who usually fills in for her is on maternity leave,' he said, correctly deducing what she was about to say.

'There must be someone else.'

'No.'

Shauna saw the stubborn set of his lean jaw. 'What about a temporary service?' she suggested tentatively.

'No way. I've gone down that rocky route before. Either you get a temp whose skills are excellent but she knows nothing about the music business or you get one who's so fascinated by the entertainment industry she forgets how to type. I'm not sure which is worse: having a secretary who thinks New Wave is something you get at a beauty salon or having one who turns into a gibbering idiot because she's asked to get Mick Jagger's manager on the phone.'

'But why me?'

'Why not?' he countered.

She could think of a great many reasons why not.

'I've already cleared this with Emmett, by the way,' he added.

She stared at him in disbelief, her eyes widening with indignation. 'Then why are we even discussing it?' she flared. 'It doesn't seem to me that I have any real choice in the matter.'

'You could always quit again,' he observed lightly. 'But the reason we're discussing it, Shauna, is that—as a matter of principle—I prefer my . . . employees to be willing.'

The slight pause before the word 'employees' triggered a peculiar fluttering in her stomach. He was so damn sure of himself. And of her, it appeared. For a moment, Shauna wondered what he'd do if she threw his 'business proposition' back in his handsome face. The desire to put a dent, no matter how small, in his galling self-confidence was almost overwhelming.

But would the momentary satisfaction of doing so be worth losing her job for? Would it be worth jeopardising the struggle for independence she'd fought so hard since her aunt died? The impulse faded as her good sense asserted itself. For one reason or another, Michael Sebastian had decided to overlook what had happened between them Friday night. She did not think his forbearance would extend to accepting a rejection of this offer.

'What—what would being your secretary involve?'

The quirk of his mobile mouth told her he'd read capitulation into the question.

'The work would be similar to the kind of thing you're doing. You may be called on to help with the care and feeding of some of SEE's more difficult clients, but I have a hunch you can handle them.'

Shauna nodded automatically. It was handling *him* she was worried about.

'The schedule will be more demanding than it is in the legal department. Will that present any problems?'

'Problems?'

'Any boyfriends or lovers who'd object to you working early hours—or late nights—with me?'

She stiffened, hot colour flooding up into her face. 'I don't really think that's any of your business,' she told him steadily. 'And if there are any problems, I'll deal with them.' There were no boyfriends—and certainly no lovers—but she was not about to admit that to him.

'Hm.' It was a neutral sound. 'Family?'

The probing bothered her. 'My parents died when I was a child,' she said starkly. 'I was raised by my father's sister in Connecticut. She's dead now, too.'

'I see. So you have no close family, then?' There was an unexpected gentleness to the question.

'No close family,' she confirmed briefly, not adding that it had been a long time—long before her aunt's death—since she'd felt that she had a family.

'OK.' He became more businesslike, easing over the sudden tension. 'I take it I've got a fill-in secretary?'

She looked at him, knowing this was her last chance to back out. Instead, with the sensation of leaping off a cliff into uncharted darkness, Shauna nodded her head once in acquiescence.

'Fine,' he smiled. 'Now, I want to talk to you about the envelope you gave me.'

She became very wary. 'That was a mistake.'

'I don't think so.'

Her eyes widened with indignation. 'You think I deliberately—' she began angrily.

'No.' He shook his head, cutting her off. 'I admit there were a few moments Friday night when I thought you might have staged the whole scene in order to get me to read your work. Don't look so surprised, Shauna. Aspiring songwriters will go to amazing lengths to get exposure for their work.'

'I suppose that's why you asked me if I was naked underneath my coat?' she demanded scathingly.

He grinned. 'I asked you if you were *dressed*,' he corrected. 'There's a big difference.'

Shauna took a shuddery breath, mentally berating herself for bringing up the incident. 'Mr Seb—'

'Michael.'

'Michael! I am *not* an aspiring songwriter! And if you actually believe I'd deliberately subject myself to the kind of humiliation—'

'I didn't say I believed it. I only said I'd thought it might be a possibility at the time. Then, of course, I decided a would-be songwriter probably wouldn't slap a record company executive across the face.'

'You know why I did—' she choked out, then stopped, forcing herself to regain her composure. It was diabolical the way this man could infuriate her! And she was going to be working with him for two weeks! She'd probably be driven to murder—or a padded cell—within two *days*.

'Yes?' he drawled, one brow raised.

'For the last time,' she said, her voice back under control and her manner a trifle rigid. 'I do not write songs.'

'OK.' He conceded the point with a shrug. 'You write lyrics.'

'I write poetry!' She caught her breath. It was the first time in her life she'd ever admitted that to anyone.

'So I've read,' he said quietly.

She swallowed convulsively. 'You had no right—'

'No right? You tossed your work in my face!'

'But I didn't mean for you to read—Besides, there's a world of difference between poetry and song lyrics.'

'Shauna, some of the best contemporary poetry around can be found in pop music lyrics.'

'You mean poetry like "ooh-ooh, baby" and "hey—"'

Michael laughed. 'You, lady, are a cultural snob.

Those "ooh-oohs" help pay your salary, you know.'

'I'm quite aware of the type of music SEE deals with,' she informed him stiffly.

'And you don't approve?'

'I didn't say that.'

'Then what are you saying?'

'I want my poetry back.' She waited for some kind of response. 'Please,' she added finally.

Michael stretched in his chair. There was a coiled spring quality to him even when he relaxed. He said nothing.

'It's—My work is private,' she said at last, making the admission in a taut voice.

'Oh, I know that.'

Something in the way he said it sent a queer sensation running through her. The unfamiliar physical awareness he evoked in her came back in full force and, with it, a renewed sense of her own vulnerability. 'What—what do you mean?'

'I mean I'm willing to bet you keep your poetry private for the same reason you wear those damn glasses and pin your hair up. I'll be honest with you. If you hadn't blown up at me in the studio the way you did, I don't think I would have believed the poetry in the envelope was yours. That calm, cool, touch-me-not routine of yours is very convincing.'

'It's not a routine,' she denied.

'It's not reality, either, if you can write the kind of poetry you do.' He leaned forward, suddenly intent. 'It must scare the hell out of you sometimes.'

He was unnervingly on the mark with his last words. There *were* moments when Shauna was deeply disturbed by the words that came spilling out of her.

'It—it's an outlet,' she conceded slowly. 'But it's personal, don't you understand? My poems aren't for public consumption.'

'They should be,' he declared flatly. 'You're good. Some of the stuff you've written practically sings itself.'

'Now you're talking about lyrics—'

He cut her off with an abrupt gesture. 'Don't start that again. If you want to think of yourself as a poet, fine. The bottom line is that with the right collaborator, I think you could be writing songs for SEE instead of typing up contracts.'

Shauna stared at him. He was serious! There was an air of creative excitement—and something else she couldn't quite read—about him. But what he was suggesting was so—

She shook her head, dispelling the momentary dreams his interest aroused. 'No, no, I couldn't. It would never work.'

'Ah, but it already has.' Michael rose in a lithe movement and crossed to the piano. He sat down, considered the keyboard with an odd, abstracted expression for a moment, then began to play.

Shauna clenched her hands together as his voice picked up the melody. There was no effort in the way he sang—no attempt to 'sell' the number. There was just an intimate blending of words and music.

It was a poem she'd written shortly after she'd come to New York: a poem full of contradictory and painful emotions. The music reflected this with aching clarity.

She stared down at her tightly interlaced fingers as Michael half-spoke, half-sang the words she knew so well:

> Some think for each, there is a lover—
> to hold them through the night.
> To keep them safe, and give them comfort,
> 'til the dark gives way to light.
> Until you find the one you're meant for . . .
>   you go through life apart.
> You are alone. You are an island—
> The keeper of an untouched heart.

Even if she'd know what to say when he finished, the words would not have come out. Her throat was dry and she could feel the pricking of tears at the corners of her eyes. A man she barely knew—a man who disturbed her on so many different levels—had gained access to a very guarded part of her life. She would have felt less revealed if he'd seen her stripped naked.

'Well?' Michael asked quietly, breaking the silence but not the tension. Shauna knew he was watching her, but she refused to look at him. She was terrified of what she might see in her face—and of what he might read in hers.

'Well, darling,' came a throaty, feminine voice from the other side of the room. 'I think it's terrific and I want to sing it.'

CHAPTER THREE

STARTLED, Shauna half-turned to face the source of the interruption. She didn't need to be told who it was. Out of the corner of her eye, she saw Michael rise from the piano, his expression guarded.

'Carla,' he said pleasantly. 'This has to be a first for you. I didn't think you got out of bed before noon.'

Carla Decker smiled. 'I don't, darling, if there's a reason to stay there.' She gave a husky laugh and strolled into the room as though she owned it.

She had a mop of dark, curly hair, creamy skin, and wide, pansy-hued eyes. The gamine effect was in contrast to the ripe, knowing curve of her mouth and the unmistakably voluptuous thrust of her very female body. She was wrapped, none too securely, in a man's towelling bathrobe. Carla was only an inch or two over five feet tall, and the garment was miles too big for her.

Shauna felt a hot flush of embarrassment colour her cheeks. That emotion gave way almost immediately to a flare of anger. How *dare* he put her in this kind of position?

Reaching Michael, Carla went up on tiptoe and kissed him, very thoroughly, on the mouth. He did not, Shauna noted with distaste, appear to object to the caress, nor to the way that Carla pressed herself up against him.

'Really, Michael,' Carla said in a mock accusatory voice, smoothing her fingertips down the front of his sweater, 'don't you ever sleep? I'd think you'd need some rest after last night. I certainly did.'

The sly innuendo made Shauna uncomfortable in the extreme. She had no doubt it was being done deliberately: Carla had to be aware there was a third person in the room.

'Carla, darling,' Michael cut in drily, 'I think you're

embarrassing my secretary-to-be.' He disengaged himself with a wry smile. 'I've had enough trouble soothing her ruffled sensibilities this morning without you coming on to the scene in your usual uninhibited style. Meet Shauna Whitney. Shauna, Carla Decker.'

Carla did not seem at all offended at being described as uninhibited, but there was a cool—even unpleasant —quality to the assessing look she gave Shauna. 'So sorry,' she drawled with sweet insincerity. Although she'd allowed Michael to put a few inches between them, she'd linked her arm possessively through his. 'I didn't see you.'

Shauna could feel herself withdrawing behind the impenetrable wall of good manners that had served her so well in the past. She had no idea why Carla Decker was going to such trouble to stake a claim on Michael Sebastian—nor did she care to find out. And she certainly had no intention of being drawn into some kind of verbal jousting match.

'That's quite all right, Miss Decker,' she said politely, standing up with quiet grace. She was acutely aware of the fact that Michael was watching her with undisguised and somewhat amused interest. 'My business with Mr Sebastian is done.'

'Oh, I wouldn't say that, Shauna,' he put in. 'As you've accepted my proposition, I'd say your business with me is just starting.'

Shauna's well-learned lessons in deportment almost went out the window with that blandly voiced remark. Then she saw the devilish light glinting in the green depths of his eyes. He was baiting her again.

'Proposition?' There was a definite edge to Carla's distinctive voice. 'But, didn't you say secretary?' She pronounced the word with barely veiled condescension.

'Yes,' Michael confirmed. 'I've seduced Shauna away from Emmett Barkley—on a temporary basis.'

'A *very* temporary basis,' Shauna clarified. She knew he was being deliberately provocative in his choice of words.

Carla's violet eyes narrowed. 'Emmett Barkley?'

'SEE's chief legal adviser,' Michael said.

Unexpectedly, Carla gave a trill of laughter. There was more than a trace of malice in it. 'Of course, now I know who she is! Outraged virtue!' She laughed again, slanting an appealing look up at Michael. His expression had gone stony. 'Don't you remember? You must! It was the day I got upset over that stupid contract clause.'

'I seem to recall your getting upset over a number of different contract clauses on a number of different occasions.'

'Don't be mean!' She pulled a small pout. 'I'm talking about the time you came and straightened everything out. Then we went down in the elevator together—' She let her voice trail off significantly.

Shauna knew precisely what Carla was talking about. It had been the first time—the only time before the previous Friday—that she'd seen Michael Sebastian in the flesh. She'd only had the job about a month and had been coming back from her lunch hour. She'd been more than a little shocked when the lift she'd been waiting for in the lobby of the SEE building slid silently open to reveal a couple locked in what could only be described as a torrid embrace.

It had been Michael Sebastian and Carla Decker and they'd gone on kissing for what seemed like an impossible period of time. Shauna had stood there, rooted to the spot.

What had been the worst thing about the incident —and in retrospect, what had made her the angriest —was that when Michael and Carla had finally broken apart, they had not been at all disturbed to discover they had an audience. In fact, judging from the gurgle of laughter Shauna heard issuing from Carla as she and Michael strolled away, they'd been monumentally amused by the whole episode.

It was only after Shauna got back up to her office that she learned what had led up to the embrace. It seemed that Carla had been causing a scene in the Legal Department when Michael, with uncanny timing, appeared. He had proceeded to calm her down by, as one admiring male witness described it, doing everything but making love to her in full view of three lawyers, her manager, several secretaries, and a miscellaneous assortment of clerical workers.

'Oh, you must remember,' Carla prompted. 'The elevator doors opened and there we were . . . and there *she* was—' She laughed again. 'The look on her face!'

'Carla, that's enough,' Michael interrupted. There was a definite edge to his voice.

The singer blinked, stroking her fingers up his arm. 'But, darling,' she said insinuatingly, 'it was funny. You said she made you understand the meaning of the phrase "outraged virtue" for the first time in your life.'

'Virtue has never been one of my strong points.' There was an oddly bitter undertone to the comment.

Carla's thinly plucked brows contracted. 'Michael—'

Michael wasn't paying any attention. 'Of course, I may have been a little hasty in my assessment, too,' he observed, his expression enigmatic as he gazed thoughtfully at Shauna.

A fine line of puzzlement appeared on Shauna's smooth forehead. She had had the strange impression in the recording studio that Michael had somehow recognised her. But she'd dismissed it as absurd. There'd been nothing memorable about her that day. Yet it seemed he *had* remembered her. Why?

And his comment about making a hasty assessment: it was such an unexpected thing for him to say. There could be an apology implicit in those words. Then again—

Then again, she didn't think she'd been hasty in her assessment of him! His behaviour at the studio—and during the past thirty minutes—confirmed her judgment that, while Michael Sebastian was undoubtedly brilliant at what he did, she did *not* like the way he did it! Probably the only reason he recalled her from the lift incident was that her hot-faced embarrassment had seemed so quaintly amusing to someone as jadedly sophisticated as he was.

She glanced pointedly at her watch. 'Mr Sebastian, I have to get back to work. And you plainly have other affairs to attend to.' Two could play the *double entendre* game! 'About my—ah—' she didn't want to say 'poetry' in front of Carla Decker.

'Your papers?' he filled in. 'I think I'll hang on to them for a bit longer. If you don't mind?'

She did mind, and she was certain he knew it. But she wasn't up to challenging him . . . not with the other woman present. She recalled what Carla had said about the song she'd overheard. The thought of having her words sung by Michael Sebastian's mistress made her sick.

'If you're certain that's what you want,' Shauna said finally, her tone as stiff as her posture.

'That's what I want,' Michael assured her, his green eyes glinting suddenly. 'For the moment.'

'Well, then—' the basic civilities struck in her throat. She'd choke if she tried to say she'd enjoyed the last half hour—or that there'd been anything remotely pleasant about meeting Carla Decker.

'Yes?' he prompted.

Shauna arranged her face into a polite expression by sheer force of will. 'Until Monday, Mr Sebastian.'

'Until Monday, Miss Whitney,' he agreed. His sudden reversion to formality carried a mixture of warning and anticipation in it. 'I look forward to working with you.'

It wasn't until Shauna got back to the office that she realised she'd not only been manoeuvred into leaving her poems with Michael, but that she'd also neglected to reclaim her glasses from him. She added that fact to the mounting list of grievances she was chalking up against her employer.

So, he was looking forward to working with her, was he? She could just imagine what he had in mind!

On second thoughts, she probably couldn't. Shrewd and experienced, Michael Sebastian undoubtedly could come up with schemes she'd never dream of in her worst nightmares and he'd have no compunction about carrying them out.

Yet this same man—this man who intimidated yet intrigued her—had composed music that caught and complemented the spirit of the words she had written. It was as though he understood . . . as if some kind of instantaneous communication had sprung up between them. On the whole, she found that more disturbing than anything else. Taken with his very potent masculine magnetism, it made him all too attractive, and she did not want to be attracted to a man like him.

Attracted! Shauna's eyes turned crystalline with inner anger as she sat down at her desk. She advised herself to abandon that course of thinking immediately. Michael Sebastian might very well have a good opinion of her secretarial skills and he might genuinely believe she had writing talent, but he'd plainly told her that, on a personal level, he thought her a prude and a snob.

Don't be an idiot, she ordered herself. You don't even like the man! All you have to do is get through two weeks of temporary work with him . . . that's all!

Naturally, word of her reassignment got around the Legal Department before the day was out, and she was subjected to a number of speculative stares and pseudo-casual questions. She ignored the stares and dealt with the questions in her usual cool but polite manner. To her relief, except for a few envious sighs from one of the filing clerks and a renewal of the flirtatious attentions of a SEE lawyer who'd tried to date her in the past, the matter seemed relegated to the dull category of old news by the end of the following day.

Then Jamie Cord strolled in and perched himself, in a very familiar fashion, on the corner of her desk.

She was so engrossed in proofing the contract she'd just finished typing that she didn't even register his presence until a small tape cassette bounced on the desk in front of her. She glanced up, eyes widening in surprise.

'Hi, Shauna,' he greeted her cheerfully, giving her a grin that was the essence of boyish charm. 'Am I interrupting something?'

'Hello, Jamie,' she responded. 'Yes, as a matter of fact, you are.'

He made an apologetic gesture and ran his hand through his shaggy brown hair in a movement that reminded Shauna of his half-brother. 'Sorry,' he said. 'I just wanted to give you that.' He pointed to the cassette. 'I had the guys at the studio dub it off for you. It's the song we did the other night, thanks to you. I thought you'd like a copy.' He unzipped the front of his leather jacket, apparently settling in for a visit.

'That was very nice of you, Jamie,' she said with a small smile. It *was* a thoughtful gesture, even if it was a reminder of an incident she'd just as soon forget. 'Thank you.'

He shrugged. 'What can I say? I'm a wonderful guy.'

'And modest, too,' she retorted.

'Well, I'm working on that,' he conceded slyly. He cocked his head, regarding her with interest. 'You look —different,' he observed. 'Hey, I know—no glasses!'

Shauna's momentary feeling of goodwill evaporated. She still hadn't got her glasses back and she'd had a number of comments about her sudden switch to contacts. Most of them had been flattering, but more than a few had held an undertone of curiosity about just what had prompted the change.

'Anything you want to say about my glasses should be directed at your brother,' she said tartly. 'He seems to have developed some kind of fetish for my property.'

Jamie looked startled. 'But, I—uh—I thought you two had kissed and made up.'

Shauna glared at him, her fine features tense. 'Is that what he said?' she demanded icily. It seemed Jamie was familiar with his half-brother's tactics for dealing with women!

'No, no, of course not,' he assured her hastily. 'It's just that—I mean, you are going to be working with him, aren't you? Filling in for Dee?'

Shauna sighed. Jamie really didn't deserve to have his head snapped off. It wasn't his fault he was related to the man who currently topped the list of people she'd least like to be stranded on a desert island with.

'I am,' she told him in a more moderate tone. 'But I'm doing it on a strictly temporary basis.'

Jamie relaxed, a mischievous look flickering in his brown eyes. 'That should be interesting.'

'I can think of other words to describe it.'

'Yeah,' he nodded understandingly, an odd expression on his face. Shauna could see definite facial similarities between Jamie and Michael, but there was still a boyish immaturity about the younger half-brother's looks. Michael's strong features bore the hammer marks of arrogance and experience; Jamie's, though confident and attractive, still seemed open to moulding.

'Jamie, I think—' She was about to suggest that she had to get back to work.

'Look, Shauna,' he interrupted. 'The real reason I stopped by was to find out if you're going to be busy this weekend.'

'I—I beg your pardon?'

'If you're not busy, I thought you could come up to Hartford.'

'Hartford?' she echoed, mystified.

He nodded. 'Right. With Tempest.'

She could feel herself start to blush. Clearly, Jamie had got the wrong idea about her. Strangely enough, she didn't feel insulted. On the other hand, if the suggestion had come from Michael—

She bit her lip. 'Jamie, I don't think so. It's not a good idea.'

'Why not?' he countered bluntly.

'Well—' She hesitated, knowing that whatever she said, it was going to come out sounding hopelessly

outmoded and probably a bit judgmental. 'I—ah—I'm
not the type—'

Jamie picked up on her anxiety almost instantly. 'Oh,
hey, no!' he exclaimed. 'This isn't a come on. I mean, I
know you're—I wasn't suggesting anything like that,
really. God, no. This is an effort to apologise.'

'Apologise?'

'Yeah. The guys—Tempest—well, we feel lousy
about what happened Friday night.'

'That wasn't the band's fault.'

'Maybe not. Then again, I was the one who made that
crack about you to begin with. And you got a rough deal
because of it. But we got some solid inspiration from
you, and we'd like to say thanks.' He paused, gauging
her reaction. 'Besides, if you're going to be in this
industry—and especially if you're going to work for
Michael—it'd be a good thing for you to see what it's like
backstage and on the road.'

There was a definite appeal to the idea, Shauna
realised. Except for one major consideration—

'Is your brother—?' she began carefully.

'He took off for London yesterday,' Jamie laughed.
'To tell the truth, I think he was glad to get out of the
country.'

'Why's that?' she asked curiously.

'Carla Decker. Do you know her?'

'We've met.'

'Well, take it from me, a little of that lady goes a long
way. Now, I can understand why Michael—uh, you
know—' he pulled a face, obviously trusting Shauna
to fill in the blank. After the little scene she'd wit-
nessed at Michael's apartment—and the one she'd
stumbled on that day in front of the lift—she, too, could
understand 'why Michael' where Carla Decker was
concerned.

'Jamie—'

'I promise you'll have a good time. It's the first concert
of the tour. You'll bring us luck, just like Friday night,'
he coaxed.

Lord, she certainly hoped nothing would ever be like Friday night!

'I have to work.'

'No problem. The concert doesn't start until eight, and with our opening act, it'll be at least nine before we get on. You finish work about four-thirty, right? I'll get a limo to pick you up and drive you—'

'A limo! Jamie, you're crazy. There are trains—'

'Ah-ha! Then you'll come!' He pounced on her words triumphantly.

'Well—' She could feel herself weakening, even though this was not the sort of thing she did. She wondered how Aunt Margaret would have reacted to the notion of her niece going off for the weekend with a group of touring rock musicians. The idea was both alarming and exhilarating.

'We'll get a hotel room for you,' he promised. His tone had become wheedling. 'You can stay over Friday, hang out with us Saturday and catch the concert that night. Then you can come back to New York Sunday. Meanwhile, Tempest heads on its merry way to—uh —Springfield, Massachusetts, I think.'

'It does sound like fun,' she admitted.

'It'll be terrific. Come on, say you'll do it. The other guys will be let down if you don't. They think you're really something after that scene in the studio.'

Shauna flushed. 'About that—'

Jamie didn't seem to notice her discomfort. 'It was pretty amazing. One minute's Michael's kissing you, the next minute you've hauled off and—'

'Jamie, I remember what happened,' Shauna cut in desperately. She'd suddenly realised that her visitor and his comments were arousing quite a bit of interest in the office. His appearance, on top of the news about her job with Michael Sebastian, was bound to generate plenty of speculation. The last thing in the world she wanted was for the department gossips to learn what had happened on Friday night.

'It's pretty hard to forget,' he went on blithely. 'I

mean, that's not usually the way women react to my big brother. But then, he doesn't usually react to them the way he reacted to you, either.' He seemed to reflect on the situation before shaking his head, refocusing on the matter at hand. 'So, will you come? Please?'

Why not? she asked herself suddenly. What harm could it do?

'All right,' she said. 'I'll do it.'

'Great! Now, about your getting up there—'

'I'll take the train,' she said firmly. 'Where exactly is your concert?'

He told her. 'You could catch a cab from the train station—'

'No problem. The auditorium is within walking distance if worst comes to worst.'

'How do you know that?'

'I grew up near Hartford.'

'No kidding! Is your family still there?'

Shauna shook her head. 'They're all dead,' she replied simply, hoping he wouldn't press her to elaborate.

He didn't. After giving her a sympathetic look, he went on. 'You're sure, now? About coming up? I don't want you to feel like you're being forced into doing something . . . like the other night.'

Somehow, it all kept coming back to that!

'Jamie, there's no comparison between my deciding to accept your invitation and what happened last Friday.'

He grinned. 'You mean, I said "please" and Michael didn't?'

'Something like that.' She was beginning to like Jamie very much. 'There is one major similarity between the two of you. Neither seems willing to take "no" for an answer.'

'True,' he agreed. 'Look, I'll leave your name with the box office and the security people so you won't have any trouble getting in, OK?'

'Thank you.'

Jamie hesitated. 'There is one more thing. It's just

that—well, um, we're all pretty casual, you know? Concerts like ours, they're nothing to get really dressed up about.' He gestured awkwardly, obviously not wanting to offend her.

Shauna smiled wryly. Although Jamie wasn't as blunt as his half-brother, the message came through loud and clear. He, too, thought she looked like somebody's stodgy maiden aunt.

'Don't worry,' she reassured him mildly. 'I won't show up looking like your mother.'

Unexpectedly, his expression hardened. 'God, I hope not,' he said flatly. 'The last time I saw her, she was running around in designer jeans trying to reclaim her lost youth.'

'Oh.' Shauna didn't know what to say. 'I—I'm sorry.'

His face cleared. 'No, I'm the one who's sorry for being so touchy. It's just that my mother isn't very maternal. Still, I shouldn't complain. At least she didn't dump me the way she dumped Mi—' he stopped abruptly.

At least she hadn't dumped him the way she'd dumped Michael, Shauna completed silently with a stirring of compassion. She kept quiet, realising that Jamie had said more than he intended.

'Never mind,' he muttered finally. 'Forget I said anything. Michael keeps telling me I have a ten-speed mouth and a half-speed mind.' He gave her a lopsided smile and jammed his hands deep into the pockets of his jacket as he got off her desk. 'Anyway. Friday in Hartford, Connecticut, right?'

Shauna nodded, responding to the hurt she sensed with a warm, sweet smile. 'Friday in Hartford.'

Despite a good many second thoughts, Shauna caught a train from Penn Station in New York to Hartford after work on Friday as she'd promised. The last time she'd been on the train had been the day she'd moved to Manhattan. She'd had a good many second thoughts on that trip, too.

To her astonishment, she was approached by a husky, long-haired young man wearing jeans, a down-filled jacket, and a single earring, almost as soon as she got off the train.

'Shauna Whitney, right?' he asked, grinning at her in a disarming manner.

'I—' She glanced around at the other passengers who were jostling by, all intent on their own affairs. 'Who—?'

'It's OK,' he assured her. 'Jamie sent me to pick you up. He wanted to make sure you got to the concert safely.'

'But he didn't know which train—'

'There aren't that many New York to Hartford trains this time of night,' he said cheerfully. 'I got here a while ago and just hung around.'

'Thank you. But it really wasn't necessary.'

'Always my pleasure to pick up a good-looking lady,' he chuckled. 'I'm Kyle, by the way.'

'Kyle. How did you know who to—pick up?'

'Easy. Jamie said to watch for a tall, classy chick with reddish-brown hair who looked like the poetry type.' He relieved her of her overnight bag.

'Poetry type?' she repeated thinly.

'Yeah, you know. Not the type of lady you'd expect to go on the road with a rock band. A symphony orchestra, maybe, but not a rock group.'

Shauna couldn't help but laugh. Then she glanced down at herself. Keeping Jamie's hint about her appearance in mind, she'd changed clothes in the ladies' room at the office before catching the train. She had on a pair of beige pinwhale corduroy jeans tucked into her brown boots and topped with a toning beige and rust sweater. She'd unpinned her hair from its customary confining knot and let it fall loose, clipping it off her face with tortoiseshell combs.

'Jamie hinted that I might not be "with it",' she confessed ruefully.

'You look fine to me,' Kyle told her warmly, giving

her a friendly wink. 'C'mon. The car's out front.'

'What do you do for Tempest?' Shauna asked once they'd got into the car.

'You mean, besides picking up incoming ladies? I'm your basic roadie. Strong back, weak mind.' He laughed amiably. 'Seriously, though, I handle equipment: set it up, check it out, break it down.'

'Have you worked with Tempest before?'

He started the engine. 'Not exactly. They did a tour before this one as the warm-up act for a band I used to work for, though, so I know what to expect. In any case, they've got a good reputation.'

'Do you like touring?'

'Going on the road is like getting married, I guess. If it works, there's nothing like it. If it doesn't—' He grimaced eloquently as he released the handbrake.

'If it doesn't—?' Shauna prompted curiously.

'In marriage, you can get divorced. If things go on the rocks on the road, either the tour goes down the drain and a bunch of people get fired, or everybody starts going crazy.'

'Does it go crazy very often?' she asked, adopting his phrase in an effort not to sound critical or naïve.

He pulled out. 'It depends. There's always booze, drugs, girls—if that's your scene. Some groups go wild on the road. It's a different city every other night and you lose track of normal life. Plus, there's the pressure of keeping up your energy level for the performance. It can get rough. SEE's known for keeping its tours pretty straight. Michael Sebastian doesn't stand for any kind of star trips from anybody. He comes down hard on troublemakers.'

'You sound as though you admire him.'

Kyle nodded. 'Absolutely.'

The drive from the station was quick thanks to a couple of hair-raising manoeuvres on Kyle's part as he navigated through the predictable Friday night traffic. Shauna felt a stab of nostalgia as she sighted a number of familiar landmarks, including the great, gold-domed state capitol building. Bathed in light, the building's remarkable pot-pourri of architectural periods and styles stood out against the night sky.

'Do you want me to let you out in front or are you coming backstage?' Kyle asked as they reached their destination.

'Out front is fine, Kyle. Jamie said he was leaving my name at the box office.'

'OK. When the show's over, duck around to the stage door in the back and tell the security guard who you are. He'll let you in.'

'Thank you.'

'My pleasure. Nice to have met you, Shauna. Enjoy the concert.'

As it turned out, Shauna did precisely that, finding herself caught up in the all-out, exhilarating show put on by Tempest. She was particularly surprised and touched when the group ended their final encore of the evening by dedicating to her a rendition of the song they'd been recording the previous Friday. To judge by the crowd's wildly enthusiastic reception, Tempest was going to have another hit on its hands.

'You deserved it,' Jamie declared afterwards as they all piled into the rented limousine that was to take them to their hotel. Despite the hour and the obvious drain of the performance, the band members were wound up tight and electric with energy.

'All I did was sit there in the studio,' Shauna laughed. She was wedged in between Jamie and Griz.

'It was the way you sat around,' Griz told her. He took a healthy swallow from the bottle of beer he was holding, then raised it in salute. 'To Shauna.'

The guitarists, Hank and Frank, were balanced on the jump seats in the back, slurping down cans of soda. They joined in the toast.

Sam Gleason, who was sitting in the front next to the driver, shifted himself around. 'That was a high compliment, Shauna,' he said. 'If anybody knows the finer points of sitting around, it's good old Griz.'

'Hey, watch it, drummer boy. My artistic genius makes me very sensitive.'

This remark was greeted by hoots of good-natured laughter. Shauna smiled, marvelling at their easy camaraderie. 'Well, I think you're all artistic geniuses,' she said. 'You were wonderful tonight and I had a marvellous time.'

'Our pleasure, ma'am,' Jamie returned with exaggerated gallantry.

The hotel they were staying at was a surprise to Shauna. She'd subconsciously associated rock tours with cut-rate highway motels. Tempest was booked into one of the priciest facilities in Hartford.

'Nice, huh?' Jamie said with a grin as the uniformed doorman assisted Shauna out of the car.

'Very impressive,' she agreed. The heavy plate-glass doors to the blue and beige lobby parted with a soft electronic hiss.

'We were lucky to get in here, actually. Besides the fact that this kind of place isn't crazy about having rock musicians as guests, there's some kind of medical convention going on and the place is totally jammed.'

Shauna was about to comment on the contrast between Tempest's very casual attire and the posh décor of the hotel when she remembered something. 'Oh, Jamie —my suitcase! Kyle took it when he met me at the train and I completely forgot about it.'

'Don't worry. Somebody brought it over here earlier. It's in your room. Speaking of which, you're all checked in. Just let me get your key from registration. I'll meet you at the elevator.' Before she could say anything, he had loped off towards the front desk. Shauna walked slowly over to the bank of lifts, joining the other members of the band. They were engrossed in a dissection of the evening's performance.

Jamie was back in under a minute, dangling a key between two fingers. He handed it to Shauna. 'Here you go. Look, are you sure you don't want to come out with us for something to eat?' he asked her.

The band had discussed the matter in the limousine. From what Shauna had gathered, Tempest made it a habit to eat out together after every performance.

'I appreciate the invitation,' Shauna said sincerely. 'But, really, it's been a long week for me and I'd like to get a good night's sleep.' She hadn't slept well since the previous weekend. 'I don't mean to be a wet blanket,' she added.

'We understand,' Jamie said with a grin. He glanced at the other four musicians. 'Twenty minutes down here in the lobby?'

'Let's synchronise our watches,' Griz suggested facetiously as the lift arrived with a soft chiming sound.

Shauna, to her surprise, was not staying on the same floor as the band. Her room was located on the top level. She let herself in with the key Jamie had given her and flicked on the light inside the door in an automatic gesture. What she saw left her momentarily speechless.

The room was a suite. Stylishly furnished in cream, blue and gold, it came complete with a small kitchenette and bar. The living room-sitting area of the place was larger than her entire apartment back in Manhattan.

If it hadn't been for the fact that her trim brown case had been placed just inside the door, she would have thought there'd been some kind of mistake made at the registration desk. She was considering this possibility when the phone rang.

The phone was located on a chrome and glass end-table that was part of a conversational grouping of furniture in the middle of the room. Crossing the blue wall-to-wall carpet, she sat down on the cream and gold patterned sofa and picked up the receiver.

'Shauna?' It was Jamie.

'Yes?'

'Just wanted to make sure you found your way. Do you like the room?'

'Like it? Jamie, you could hold a mass rally in here! It's absolutely gorgeous, but I don't need anything this elaborate.'

'It's all they had available. Like I said, the place is packed because of the medical convention. Still, I promised you a room, didn't I?'

'But something like this?' She shuddered as she imagined the nightly rate on this sort of accommodation. 'Jamie, I had no idea—'

'You deserve the best,' he said quickly. 'Tempest owes you. Besides—' he chuckled, 'SEE's picking up the tab.'

'SEE? Oh, no!' That upset her.

'Shauna, Shauna, it's OK, believe me. Just forget your worries and enjoy yourself. Please.'

'Well . . .' She nibbled her lower lip. Trying to find another room at this time of night would be awkward to say the least. And she had the feeling Tempest would be offended if she rejected their gesture of hospitality. Still, she was uncomfortable with the idea of staying anywhere this elaborate—especially when the company she worked for was paying the bill.

'Shauna?' He sounded both coaxing and anxious.

'It's a beautiful room,' she said finally. 'If this is a sample of life on the road, I could get to like it,' she added, resolutely shutting her mind to her misgivings. She could always find some discreet way of reimbursing SEE . . .

'Great. Sleep tight. If you want anything, I'm in Room 912.'

'Good night, Jamie. And thank you.'

Fighting back a yawn, Shauna stood up and retrieved her suitcase. With an almost overwhelming sense of weariness tugging at her, she carried the bag into the bedroom. It was on the same elegantly enormous scale as the rest of the suite. The bed itself, already invitingly turned down for the night, was huge.

She hummed as she prepared for bed, breaking off once with an uneasy start as she realised she'd begun singing the tune Michael Sebastian had played for her at his apartment. She wanted to forget she'd ever heard that piece of music. She also wanted to forget she'd heard Carla Decker say she wanted to sing it. The head of Sebastian Entertainment Enterprises was free to give his mistress the melody, but she was never going to get the words! Those belonged to Shauna, and they weren't meant to be shared.

Clad in her nightgown, her hair flowing in chestnut waves over her shoulders and her pale face cleansed and moisturised, Shauna went back out into the living room and turned out the lights. Returning to the bedroom, she drew the heavy curtains on the window shut. She got into the enormous bed and, stifling another yawn, reached over and switched off the bedside lamp. Pulling the bed linen over her, she snuggled down with an exhausted sigh.

Ten minutes later, her face very innocent in the darkness, she was sound asleep.

CHAPTER FOUR

SHAUNA was dreaming. It was a vivid, strangely pleasurable dream. She felt so soft and yielding . . . so protected and cherished. She was being held, cocooned in an erotic but seductively secure cradle of warmth.

It was like being enchanted back to the embraces of her early childhood, with one heady difference: this embrace stirred her awareness of her body and its femininity—its needs.

She made a throaty, yearning little sound and shifted, wanting to move closer to the source of this voluptuous comfort.

And then she wasn't dreaming anymore. But something—*someone!*—was still holding her.

Her pleasure dissolved in the onslaught of two intensely contradictory emotions: white-hot fury and cold, heart-clutching fear. Someone was in bed with her!

Shauna went rigid. She drew a shaky breath, intending to scream, but in the split second before she could force the sound out, there was a muttered curse and an abrupt movement beside her. The bedside lamp flared on.

The scream died in her throat as her eyes adjusted to the light. It took her mind a few moments longer to adjust to—and accept—what she was seeing.

The 'someone' in bed with her was Michael Sebastian. He was half-sitting up, looming over her like some diabolically sensual nightmare summoned up by her subconscious. His thick, dark hair was disordered and his heavy-lidded eyes held a disconcerting mixture of shock and arousal. The tanned, leanly muscled lines of his upper body were highlighted by the glow of the lamp, underscoring the pagan quality of his masculinity. One involuntary glance downward informed Shauna that he was wearing little—if anything at all—beneath the protective covering of the bedclothes. The warmth she had been enjoying so uninhibitedly only a few moments before had clearly been the warmth of his superbly male body. It was a warmth she could still feel on the curve of one hip, where his long-fingered, musician's hand—

Gasping, Shauna jerked away from the contact, her heart pounding. 'Don't touch me!' she hissed as she sat up, clutching the sheet against her.

'Why not?' he enquired mildly. 'Don't you like being touched?' The shock she had detected in his jade green gaze was fading; in its place was an expression too complex for Shauna to try to puzzle out. While he appeared completely alert, there was an attractive, just-woken huskiness to his voice.

'Don't I like—' She could barely get the question out. Please, she thought, please, let this be a dream! But even as she made the mental plea, she knew it was futile. Michael Sebastian's presence in her bed at this moment was no more a dream than the sensations she had been experiencing only a few seconds before—sensations that had left her nerve endings quivering. 'How dare you!'

'How dare I what? Touch you? It seems to me you left yourself open to that sort of thing, Miss Whitney, by crawling into my bed—'

'Your bed!?' For a moment, her outrage was so great she was afraid she might strangle on the furious words that were bubbling up inside her before she could get them out. A hectic, feverish colour stained her cheeks. 'I did not crawl—this is not your bed, Mr Sebastian! It's mine! You're the one who c-crawled in where you don't belong. As for liking you touching me—I'd rather let a-a-a snake slither over me!' This kind of emotional explosion was alien to Shauna, but she found it impossible to react to Michael in a rational, controlled manner. That terrified her more than anything else, and it goaded her onward. 'I want you to get out! Do you hear me? Get out! If you don't—'

'You'll scream? Call the manager?'

'Yes!' But even as she said it, she knew something was terribly wrong. Her venomous diatribe was having no effect on him. In fact, aside from his apparent disorientation in the first confusing seconds, he actually seemed to be enjoying himself.

'Terrific,' he said. Then, to her utter dismay, he smiled. 'It should be very interesting to hear you explain what you're doing in a hotel room registered in my name, sitting in a bed my company happens to be paying for.'

Shauna felt the blood drain out of her face. What he was saying was—

'That c-can't be—' she stammered. 'Jamie said—'

'Jamie? What the hell does he have to do with this?'

'I—he—' She couldn't think straight. Nothing in a decade of stern-voiced lectures from her Aunt Margaret —or in her months of independent living in Manhattan —had remotely prepared her to deal with a situation like this.

She had to get away from him. She had to escape—

Even before the thought was completed, Michael caught her, pinning her up against the headboard of the bed. She could feel the imprint of his fingers burning into every cell of her flesh.

'Oh, no, my sweet little bundle of contradictions,' he said silkily. 'You can't run and you can't hide from me. I want some explanations. What about Jamie?'

Shauna swallowed, not daring to struggle. His lightning quick grab for her had made his nudity appallingly evident. 'I—He invited m-me up to Hartford for the concert. The Tempest concert,' she added unnecessarily, trying to keep her gaze fixed on the bridge of his nose.

'Jamie asked you to spend a weekend on the road with him and you end up sleeping with me?'

Unwisely, she replied with the first thing that popped into her head. 'He said you were going to London.' Realising the way this sounded as the words came out, she went scarlet with mortification. 'Oh—'

'While the boss is away, the employees will play—on company money?'

'No!' He had her completely rattled now. 'I wasn't —that's not what I meant! Oh, God, what kind of person do you think I am?'

It was a desperately unhappy question.

There was a long pause. Michael regarded her intently, his dark brows drawn together. Then, abruptly, he released her.

'What kind of person do I think you are?' he echoed. 'That, sweetheart, is what I'm trying to figure out. I suggest you avert your eyes. I'm getting out of bed and putting on my trousers.'

Gasping at his calm audacity, Shauna none the less turned her head. She felt the mattress give as he got up. Fighting down a sudden, shocking urge to take one small glance, she kept her eyes carefully focused on the floor even after she heard the sound of a zipper closing.

'You can look now,' he said drily. 'I'm partially dressed if not basically decent.'

She turned back, strangely shy. He was wearing a pair of jeans that were as form-fitting as the ones he'd had on back at his apartment. He sat down on the edge of the bed.

'OK.' He drew the word out on a sigh. Shauna realised he looked very tired. 'Let's take it from the top. You came to Hartford with Jamie for the weekend.'

'I came up to see Tempest play a concert,' she corrected, trying to keep her voice steady. 'Jamie did invite me, but he said it was on behalf of the whole band. B-because of what happened last Friday in the studio.' She paused for a moment, wondering what kind of reaction that might detonate. She slanted a look at Michael, but he simply nodded. 'He said . . . he said it was a gesture of apology.'

'And you believed him?'

'Yes!' Although he didn't show it, she was certain he was laughing at her. 'Jamie's been very nice to me. A perfect gentleman.'

'Unlike some people you could name, right?' he gibed. 'So, fine. You accept Jamie's proposition—excuse me, Tempest's invitation—and you come up to Hartford. How did you get into this particular room?'

'With a key.'

'The desk gave you the key?'

'Not exactly. Jamie picked it up for me after the concert—' She stopped, her eyes widening as an awful thought struck her. 'You think Jamie arranged this?' Her voice rose starkly and she started to tremble.

'Take it easy,' he said firmly, catching her by the shoulders.

'You think he put me in here for you?'

'No!' His voice was sharp. 'God, no.' There was something alarmingly introverted about his expression.

'M-Michael?' It was such an odd look—

He shook his head as though to clear it. 'Jet lag. I should have figured that something like this—I thought it was Dee and her pre-honeymoon haze again.'

'I don't understand.' Bewildered as she was, Shauna was still acutely conscious of the warm curve of his palms resting on her shoulders.

Astonishingly, he gave her a crooked grin. 'No, I don't suppose you do. And four o'clock in the morning in a hotel room is a hell of a time and place to take your education in hand.' He stroked down her upper arms then let go of her, expelling a deep breath. 'OK. Here's what I think happened. I was in London this week, just like Jamie said. But I was scheduled to fly back to the States to catch the kick-off of Tempest's tour.'

'Then this suite—'

'Was reserved for me, but not until Saturday.'

'W-what?'

'I got through early in London, so I decided to change my flight and come into Hartford earlier than planned. Unfortunately, there were weather problems at Heathrow and we were about four hours late taking off. By the time I finally got here to the hotel, I was ready to beg, borrow, or steal a place to crash for a couple of hours.

SONG WITHOUT WORDS   71

You can imagine my surprise when the front desk happily informed me they were already holding a suite in SEE's name. I assumed Dee mixed up the dates. Falling in love has had that kind of effect on her efficiency. What I think now is that my enterprising younger brother decided to piggyback you on to the company bill for tonight. What he intended to do with you for the rest of the weekend is open to speculation.' His brows quirked up.

Shauna felt herself flush, but refused to respond to what she sensed was a deliberate attempt to provoke her. 'Then you don't think Jamie meant for you and me—?'

He shook his head. 'As much as he has to answer for in this little fiasco, I'll acquit him of that. Of course, you aren't entirely blameless in this affair, Miss Whitney.'

She swallowed. 'The hotel bill?' she guessed guiltily. 'I'll reimburse SEE, of course, but I—'

'Forget the bill,' he advised tersely. 'I'm talking about the act that I was able to get into the suite while you were in it. Do you make it a habit to ignore elementary safety precautions like throwing the dead bolt and putting on the chain lock?' There was a sudden snap of temper in his eyes.

Shauna's hand came up to her mouth. 'I didn't—'

'No, you didn't,' he said incisively.

'I—I suppose I wasn't thinking . . . but—' Her chin tilted as her air of embarrassed apology dissolved in a sudden wave of indignation. 'But you're still the one who got into bed with me!' she accused.

'Hold it. I did not get into bed with you—at least not intentionally.'

'Oh, really? I suppose you didn't notice me?'

'As a matter of fact, I did not. I was dead on my feet when I got here. I dumped my bags, stripped down, got into bed, and went to sleep. I did not turn on the bedroom light. I did not see you. I didn't even *feel* you—'

'You felt plenty!' she snapped rudely.

'I'm talking about when I first—Look, Shauna, this damn bed is the size of a football field! You were probably huddled up on the right side of the mattress when I fell asleep on the left.'

'Unfortunately, you didn't stay there,' she reminded him.

'You weren't exactly observing strict territorial boundaries, either.'

'But I wasn't—doing what you were doing.'

'And just what was I doing? All I know is that one minute I was having a perfectly enjoyable dream and the next I was being jerked awake—'

'You're saying you were asleep when you—you were practically m-making love—'

'Shauna.' His expressive eyes went brilliant with amusement. 'When I make love, there's no "practically" about it. And I can promise you, if that's what we'd been doing, both of us would have been wide awake for the experience.' A slow, knowing smile curved his lips sending a tremor through her. 'To say nothing of the fact that I'd have had that thing off you early on in the proceedings.'

That 'thing' was Shauna's nightdress. Made out of white cotton, with a high, lace-ruffled collar and long sleeves, it had an old-fashioned modesty about it; in fact, she'd discovered it in a small shop that specialised in copying antique clothing.

'Not that the Victorian virgin image doesn't suit you,' he went on with silken mockery. 'All that repression . . . But holding back can be more of a come-on than black lace and an invitation, you know. A woman puts up her hair and most men immediately start to think about taking it down. She covers herself up—'

'That's enough!' she started to edge away, shaken to the core by his insinuations.

'No, my private little poetess, it's not,' he said and reached for her, his handsome face suddenly grim.

The brief, barely exploratory kiss he had given her in the studio was nothing compared with the slow, expertly sexual assault he directed at her now. Only it wasn't really an assault . . . seducing and sharing, the mouth that moved over hers was compelling in its searching gentleness. The hands that slipped up her arms to cup her face were deliberately caressing. Force would have triggered her instant and instinctive resistance, and he was experienced enough to realise this. But in her innocence, she had no defence against an attacker who gave as much as he took.

Making himself lord of her already disordered senses, he guided her into surrender even before she recognised the nature of the fight. Responsiveness blossomed out of the surrender, flowering up inside her like some fiery, exotic bloom. She had summoned up the vague outer edges of this eated urgency once or twice in her writing . . . but the reality was beyond mere poetry.

Later—much later—she asked herself with a sense of shame how far she would have allowed him to take her if she hadn't been shocked out of the sensual dream he was spinning by the totally unfamiliar sensation of his hand closing possessively over one of her breasts. The burgeoning of her flesh against his palm seemed to set off some deeply ingrained warning system and she stiffened, feeling herself teeter on the brink even as she began to rebel.

'No,' she moaned, twisting in panic at the treachery of her own body. She had to evade his all too knowing touch . . . to deny the wellspring of desire he'd tapped with such unerring skill.

'Shauna—' His voice was thick . . . hoarse.

'Michael—' His name came out raggedly. 'Oh, please, don't—I can't—Please, help me—'

Whether it was the words or the way she said them that affected him, she didn't know. But he stilled suddenly, then released her with an oath. The gold flecks in his eyes were like molten metal and his breathing was uneven. She stared at him with frightened uncertainty.

'God, I must be out of my mind,' he said with a kind of brutal derision. Although she flinched at the harshness of his tone, she sensed somehow that the suppressed bitterness she detected in his words was directed at himself—not her. He took a deep breath and expelled it, running one hand savagely through his hair. He took another breath, bringing himself under control by sheer, visible force of will. 'Don't look at me like that, Shauna,' he ordered tautly. 'Those damned innocent eyes of your are like mirrors, reflecting the worst in me. It's not very pleasant to look at.'

'I—I'm sorry,' she stammered.

'No, I'm the one who's sorry.' He gave an ominous smile. 'And I can think of one other person who's going to be sorry.'

Shauna shivered a little. He didn't sound angry, exactly, just dangerously determined. 'You m-mean Jamie?'

Emerald-ice eyes met anxious hazel ones for a long moment. 'Are you worried about what I might do to him?' Michael asked. 'Why? His little stunt ended up with us—now how did you put it?—"practically making love".'

Shauna dropped her lashes and shifted a little, uncomfortably conscious of his scrutiny. The mockery that edged his quotation of her words didn't help. No wonder he'd taunted her about being the Victorian virgin type! Summoning up her nerve, she steeled herself to look at him again.

'Yes . . . well, practically isn't actually d-doing it, is it?' she asked in what she hoped was a reasonably adult tone. 'Besides—'

'Yes?'

'If you hadn't changed your schedule and I hadn't forgotten to lock the door properly, nothing would have happened.' She managed a rueful little smile.

His eyes narrowed. 'Oh, something would have happened, Miss Whitney,' he declared flatly. 'Just not so quickly.' He paused, then gestured dismissively as she opened her mouth to object to this very peculiar remark.

'What do you—' she began, her eyes widening.

'Look,' he cut her off. 'We're both tired. And, as I said before, four o'clock in the morning in a hotel room isn't a setting that's conducive to rational discussions between a man and woman . . . as we've been proving. I'm going to sack out for what's left of the night on the sofa in the other room. Lord knows, I've bedded down in a lot less comfortable places in my life. Unless, of course, you have some problem being in the same suite as I am?'

Shauna clenched her fists. Logic—if nothing else —demanded she accept his proposal . . . even if the way he put it made it sound like a *fait accompli* rather than a suggestion. When all was said and done, this *was* his suite. He *was* paying for it. And he was doing the gentlemanly thing. Although, when Michael Sebastian was involved, even gentlemanly behaviour had its unsettling aspects.

'No, I don't mind,' she said. 'Do you want a pillow?' There were four on the bed. She picked one up and handed it to him.

'Thank you,' he said politely, getting up off the bed. His expression was enigmatic as he nodded his leave and turned towards the door.

'Michael—'

He stopped. Slowly, almost reluctantly, he glanced back at her. Something in his eyes made her pulse start to pound with alarming rapidity. Whatever she intended to say—if she had, indeed, meant to speak at all— vanished from her mind.

'I—N-nothing,' she stuttered breathlessly.

'Nothing?'

'Just—good night.'

His lips curved. 'It has been a good night,' he observed cryptically. 'At least now I'm absolutely certain you wrote that poetry. Sleep well, Shauna—and sweet dreams.'

It took Shauna a very long time to get back to sleep after Michael left. She could still sense his presence in the room . . . even in the bed with her. And she could still feel the touch of his hands on her skin and the demanding caress of his mouth on her tender lips.

Shauna had never known a man intimately. She'd never been tempted in that direction in fact. Aunt Margaret's strict upbringing had a great deal to do with it, but her own basic emotional insecurities contributed as well. In recent years, she'd sometimes wished she could emulate the light-hearted freedom she saw other girls enjoying, but she knew, deep down, it was impossible. Casual sex was not for her. In order to give herself to a man, Shauna would need to feel a lifetime commitment . . . she would need to feel love.

Yet she had responded to Michael Sebastian—a man she scarcely knew, much less liked—and responded to him with passionate intensity. He stirred her emotionally as well as physically, evoking a response she hadn't realised she was capable of making. He touched the secret places of her soul as skilfully as she instinctively knew he would touch the secret places of her body, and it frightened her.

It frightened her because she realised she wanted him to touch her . . . she also wanted to touch him.

But that was impossible. She didn't know where to begin, and even if she did . . .

Exhausted, she finally drifted off into a restless slumber, curling up like a hurt child beneath the covers. It was a deep sleep, but a sleep troubled by disturbing snatches of dreams.

The twisted, disordered condition of the bedclothes testified to her emotional turmoil when Michael entered the room several hours later. There was a curiously guarded expression on his face as he stood by the bed, watching her silently for nearly a minute. Michael had learned to hide his own vulnerabilities at a very early age, and if he had had trouble sleeping, he gave no sign of it.

The hem of Shauna's nightdress had ridden up revealingly during her restless turnings, leaving a slender, creamy length of leg exposed. With an odd smile,

Michael leaned over and gently tugged the gown down until she was modestly covered once again. Then, with a small shrug, he went into the bathroom and closed the door.

Shauna stirred a little while later as an insistent ringing penetrated her slumberous state. It was a jangled, discordant sound that nagged through her nervous system without fully awakening her.

She groaned protestingly, but to no avail. The shrill, demanding noise continued even as she sought to ignore it. Shauna burrowed her head against the pillow. The sound went on.

'Oh, all right,' she said, opening sleep-clouded eyes. She sat up groggily, trying to force back a shuddery yawn with little success.

She glanced around. For a few awful seconds—she could practically time them by the thudding of her heart—she had absolutely no idea where she was or how she'd got there. Everything was unfamiliar. There was a closing-in rush of childhood dread; she'd known this feeling all too well in the first months after her parents' deaths when she'd woken up in the middle of the night in her bedroom in her Aunt Margaret's stiff, strange house.

Then she remembered. In a way, what she recalled was almost worse than the disorientation and the confusion. Dear Lord, had she—? And had Michael—?

She pressed a trembling hand to her face, feeling the tell-tale heat of a blush. Her long, loose hair was tumbled in wild disorder and she brushed at the chestnut tresses distractedly. She vaguely registered the sound of running water coming from the direction of the bathroom. Did that mean—

If only the telephone would stop ringing!

'The telephone!' she exclaimed. She realised the instrument was just about jumping off the hook on the stand beside the bed. Pausing long enough to click on the bedside lamp, she picked up the receiver with unsteady fingers and murmured an uncertain greeting.

There was no reply. Shauna thought she heard an angry intake of breath on the other end, but she wasn't sure.

'Hallo?' she repeated hesitantly.

'Who is this?' The question crackled through the line in a throaty, imperious tone, implying that, whomever she was, she had no business answering this phone.

'Th-this is Shauna Whitney. I—ah—' The water in the bathroom had been shut off.

'Shauna—?' There was no mistaking the unpleasantness of the tone. 'I want to speak to Michael. Right now. I know he's there. Tell him it's Carla.'

The last sentence was unnecessary. As inefficiently as her mind was performing at the moment, Shauna had already correctly deduced the caller's identity. Her momentary resentment of the singer's rudeness was lost in an upsurge of infuriated embarrassment. Here she was, in Michael Sebastian's hotel room, blithely answering a phone call from his girlfriend! And she wasn't even dressed!

Michael wasn't dressed either when he sauntered casually out of the bathroom. He was wearing nothing but a towel knotted low around his lean hips. The white of the towelling contrasted vividly with the smooth bronze of his skin. He was briskly rubbing his moisture-spangled hair with a second towel.

Again, Shauna was struck—and shaken—by his effortlessly virile charisma. She felt shy and strangely excited at the same time.

There was a classic power about his well-proportioned body that reminded her of a highly trained endurance athlete—a distance runner or a swimmer. The impact of his compelling physical appeal was heightened by his apparent nonchalance about it.

Michael stopped drying his dark hair and slung the second towel around his neck. He gave her a lazily charming smile.

Shauna's first impulse was to gather the bedclothes

around her for protection. Then she recalled his remarks about the provocative qualities of modesty and she controlled the urge.

'Good morning,' Michael said, his voice resonant and pleasant. Except for a small, teasing glint in his green eyes, there was nothing in his manner that indicated anything out of the ordinary had ever passed between them. In fact, there was nothing to indicate he found anything unusual about their current situation.

Shauna summoned up her defences, but she was unprepared to respond to this type of urbane civility. Caught off-guard, her natural courtesy triumphed over caution.

'G-good morning,' she answered, gazing at him wide-eyed. Common sense warned her that a polite, well-mannered Michael Sebastian might turn out to be the most dangerous Michael Sebastian of all. 'What are you—'

'Is that Michael?' Carla's voice jerked her abruptly back to reality. Shauna started to colour, her delicate features tightening.

'Private call?' Michael enquired blandly, one brow going up slightly. 'I can leave.'

'I want to speak to him!'

Shauna pulled the phone away from her ear and extended it to Michael. 'It's for you,' she informed him with cool distaste. 'Carla Decker.'

He took the receiver with a nod and sat down on the edge of the bed. She caught the faint scent of his subtly spicy aftershave.

A rush of words—unintelligible—issued from the phone.

'And good morning to you, too, Carla,' Michael said eventually, shifting his position. The towel he had wrapped around him hiked up as he did so, baring a hair-roughened expanse of rock hard thigh.

'What?' he questioned. 'No, you heard right.' He laughed. 'Well, babe, what do you think she's doing here?' There was a pause. Michael studied Shauna consideringly. 'Not necessarily,' he said. 'She's full of surprises.'

That did it! Thoroughly nettled by his no doubt deliberately double-edged banter, Shauna scrambled off the other side of the bed, not caring that she revealed more than a discreet flash of leg in her haste. She stalked angrily into the bathroom he had just vacated, slamming the door shut behind her.

'What is the matter with me?' she demanded in a goaded undertone, confronting her reflection in the mirror. 'I've got to stop letting him affect me like this!'

Did she affect him at all? The question crept into her mind unbidden. That her poetry intrigued him in a professional sense, she was willing to accept. As for anything else . . . it had to be a simple matter of proximity and Michael's strongly sexual nature. Perhaps he did find something perversely attractive about her naïveté and his ability to overcome her characteristic restraint. It was a cat-and-mouse game for him, no doubt—a diversion. But, in the long term, cats stuck with their own kind. Mice were only their victims.

Shauna sighed. Escaping into the bathroom had been ill-considered. Once again, she'd let him get to her. She'd also boxed herself in. She was stuck in the bathroom wearing nothing but her nightgown and she had no intention of walking out until she was positive Michael was gone.

She decided to take a shower. Slipping off her nightdress, she caught a look at herself in the mirror. With a curious feeling in the pit of her stomach, she paused to study her image more closely. What she saw was a cameo-classic face atop a slender figure.

She'd lost a few pounds over the last week, and it showed in the faint hollowing of her cheeks. That hollowing, along with the slight, smudgy shadows beneath her long-lashed hazel eyes, gave a new fragility to her looks.

The weight loss had also slimmed an inch or so off her already narrow waist. That, she saw, seemed to emphasise the gentle curves of her hips and the delicate fullness of her rose-tipped breasts. Still, she thought with a wry grimace, her figure was downright boyish when compared with Carla Decker's voluptuous femininity. She wondered if Michael—

An irritated exclamation passed her lips as she pivoted away from her eflection. Why did every line of thinking have to lead back to him? And why in heaven's name should she compare her body with Carla Decker's?

Shauna turned the shower on full blast. After gathering her tumble of hair up underneath the plastic cap provided by the hotel, she stepped into the pulsing spray. Under different circumstances, she would have found the warm, luxurious feel of the water soothing. This time she was conscious only of her agitation and her desire to scrub herself clean.

Damn Michael Sebastian! And damn his half-brother, too, for good measure! Shauna had already made up her mind to get away from Hartford and back to Manhattan that very day but, before she left, she wanted to have a few words with Jamie Cord.

She soaped herself thoroughly then rinsed off, finishing with a quick jet of cold water. Stepping carefully out of the shower, she reached for a towel. She had just finished blotting her skin dry when there was a knock on the door.

'Shauna?'

She froze, clutching the towel to her as though it was a protective shield. She'd forgotten to lock the bathroom door! All he had to do was—

'Don't come in here!'

'Don't worry,' he replied. 'I'm leaving now. I thought you might like to know so you don't feel obliged to stay holed up in the bathroom all day in your nightgown.' Shauna gritted her teeth, sure she heard a chuckle. 'I'm going to talk to Jamie. You can have the pieces afterwards.'

CHAPTER FIVE

SHAUNA finished dressing and repacking about forty-five minutes later. Gone were the loose hair and casual clothing. Her neatly groomed chignon was back in place and she'd donned a grey flannel skirt and a matching crew-neck sweater layered over a buttoned-down white Oxford-cloth shirt. A light application of make-up banished all traces of her turbulent night. She was herself again—back in control.

She phoned Jamie's room but got no answer. As she was debating what to do next, her stomach gurgled and she suddenly realised she was hungry. Except for a few odds and ends she'd snacked on backstage after the concert, she hadn't eaten since late afternoon the day before. She made another unsuccessful call to Jamie's room then decided to go downstairs to the hotel coffee shop. Perhaps she'd find him there . . .

As it turned out, he found her. She was sitting alone at a table by the window reading a fulsome review of the Tempest concert in a copy of the local paper while she waited for her breakfast order to arrive when she realised someone was standing at her elbow.

It was Jamie. The expression on his face held equal parts of embarrassment and apology. Involuntarily, Shauna glanced about, looking for Michael. He was nowhere to be seen.

'Hi,' Jamie said tentatively. 'Are you—uh—talking to me?'

'I don't think you'd enjoy what I want to say to you.' It was the kind of cool, distant tone her aunt had used on her.

Jamie winced. 'I deserve that. I guess I goofed up, huh?'

'What do you think?' she retorted then sighed, suddenly tired of the whole thing. 'Oh, never mind. It doesn't really matter.'

'Come on, sure it does!' he said quickly. 'Look . . . can I sit down?'

Reluctantly, she nodded once. He slid quickly into the seat opposite her. There was a silence as both of them fiddled with their silverware.

'I am sorry,' he said finally. 'I invited you up here because I think you're a special lady and I wanted you to have a good time. After I asked you to come, I found out the hotel was booked up. The only thing I could get for last night was the suite.' He made a doleful face. 'Everything would have been just fine if Michael hadn't shown up ahead of schedule.'

His obvious misery touched Shauna, but she wasn't ready to forgive him. 'You led me to believe he wasn't going to show up at all,' she reminded him. 'When I asked you, you said he was in London.'

'We-ell . . . actually, I said he'd *left* for London. You inferred—'

'You implied!'

'Yeah, OK, I did,' he admitted. 'I was afraid you'd turn me down if you knew he was going to be here.'

'I would have.'

'So, you see—' He spread his hands.

'Just what did you think would happen when he did show up?'

He drummed his fingers on the table. 'I was hoping you'd be having such a terrific time you wouldn't mind. I was going to arrange for another room . . . someplace—'

'Oh, Jamie!'

'Well, you are going to work with him, right?' he defended himself. 'And even though you didn't—ah —hit it off, I thought everything was straightened out.' He paused. Shauna remained silent. 'I know last night was a mess,' he went on unhappily. 'Michael said—'

Shauna paled. 'What did he say?'

'He said you'd forgotten to throw the bolt, so he didn't

realise anyone was in the suite until he turned on the light in the bedroom and woke you up.' Jamie studied her curiously. 'That is . . . Michael . . . er—Nothing happened, did it?' he asked hesitantly.

Shauna bit her lip. She supposed by Michael's sophisticated standards—and probably by Jamie's as well —nothing had happened. But by hers . . .

'No, Jamie,' she said quietly. 'Nothing happened.'

He looked relieved. 'I didn't really think so. Michael wouldn't—'

At that point, a pastel-uniformed waitress bustled up with Shauna's food. She served it deftly then asked if Jamie wanted anything. After taking his massive breakfast order, she served him a steaming cup of black coffee then moved off.

'So,' Jamie said, taking a gulp of the dark brew. 'Everything's OK now, right? Michael's going to double up with me and you can keep the suite. Nobody has to know anything—'

Shauna opened her mouth to tell him that she wouldn't need the suite because she wasn't staying when an appalling realisation struck her.

'Somebody already knows,' she moaned. 'Carla Decker called Michael's room this morning. I was half-asleep and I answered the phone.'

To her surprise, Jamie gave a snort of laughter. 'S-sorry—' he sputtered. 'I'm not laughing at you. I was just thinking about the Divine Decker phoning Michael and getting another woman. She must have thrown a fit.' He seemed inordinately pleased with the notion.

'Jamie, she knows it was me on the other end of the line! Don't you understand? What are people going to think? Especially—especially since I'm supposed to fill in as Michael's secretary starting Monday. You *know* what kind of gossip this will cause.' She rested her forehead in the palm of one hand.

'Hey, Shauna—' He reached across the table and took her other hand. 'It's all right. There's no way Carla's going to mention anything to anybody about the call.'

'How can you say that?' She disengaged her fingers from his.

'Simple. Carla and Michael are a hot and heavy item at the moment. She's not going to let it get around that another woman was in his hotel room answering his phone. She'd look like a fool.'

'And what would I look like?'

Jamie frowned. 'Yeah . . . well, I see what you mean.'

His food arrived then, and there was another break in the conversation. Jamie ate his breakfast with diligent gusto. Shauna nibbled at a piece of toast. She devoutly hoped that Jamie's prediction about Carla Decker keeping quiet would prove accurate.

Jamie crunched down a piece of bacon, studying her narrowly. 'So, do you think you might consider accepting my apology for last night?' He adopted an earnestly appealing expression. 'Forgive me, please? Pretty please?'

His manner was so coaxingly hangdog that Shauna couldn't quite suppress a smile. He was outrageous! But it was difficult to stay angry with him. For all his exaggerated woe, she sensed Jamie was sincere in his regret over the previous evening's turn of events.

'Oh . . . You're forgiven,' she told him. 'Provided you promise never to do anything like what you did again.'

'Cross my heart,' he said instantly, matching deed to words. 'After the way Michael reamed me out, I'm going to dedicate myself to winning good conduct medals for the rest of my life.'

'What did Michael say to you?' Shauna asked after a moment, her curiosity getting the better of her. He'd obviously given Jamie a highly edited version of what had happened in the suite, and for this she was grateful. But she couldn't help wondering what else he'd said.

'You wouldn't want to know,' Jamie said ruefully. 'It was almost as bad as seven years ago. I've still got the scars from that scene.'

'What happened seven years ago?'

'I got busted,' he said simply. 'Drugs.'

She couldn't hide her shock. 'I—I had no idea. I'm sorry.'

'So was I. Especially after Michael got through with me.'

'Michael? But what about your parents—' She stopped, biting her lip. 'I apologise. I shouldn't have asked that.'

'It's OK,' he assured her. 'I'd like to tell you.'

'Jamie, you don't have to—'

'I really would like to tell you,' he repeated. 'You know Michael and I are just half-brothers, don't you? Same mother, different fathers. Michael was raised by his dad. He was a musician. Not very successful, I guess. Always travelling with pick-up bands. But he cared enough about Michael to keep him with him after his wife—uh—walked out. He kept one step ahead of the child welfare people until he died of a heart attack. Michael was sixteen. Sixteen going on thirty-six in a lot of ways.'

Shauna nodded, her hazel eyes cloud-soft with sympathy.

'Michael came to live with us then, in Chicago. It was a pretty tense time for everybody. Of course, I was just a kid. Funny thing was, I liked him right from the start. He closed himself off from everybody else, but he used to play his guitar for me . . . music he'd written, songs he'd heard on the radio. Sometimes he'd tell me about all the places he'd been with his father. He'd made it sound like a big adventure, lots of fun. But looking back now, I can see it must have been rough on him . . .' He shook his head, momentarily lost in memories.

'What happened?' Shauna probed gently.

'A few days after his seventeenth birthday, he split. He picked up the stuff he'd come with—his guitar and a crummy old suitcase—and just left. My parents called the police, but they couldn't do much. We didn't know what had happened to him until about six years later when "You Made Me What I Am" came out. Do you remember that song?'

'Yes.' It had been a monumental hit the year it had been released and had triggered Michael Sebastian's meteoric rise. He'd used the leverage of suddenly being one of the hottest songwriters in the business to cut a deal with a small—some believed failing—record company. Eighteen months later, the label was thriving and Michael owned the place. He had been all of twenty-five.

'The first time I heard it on the radio, I couldn't believe it,' Jamie continued. 'I only had to hear the first few bars and I knew the song was his.'

'But how?'

'It was one of the tunes he used to play for me. They stuck in my head, even the ones without words. I always had this feeling that a lot of that music was very special to him . . . his way of letting things out he wouldn't say out loud.' He sighed. 'About four months after "You Made Me What I Am" came out, my dad got killed in an accident at work. So, it was just my mother and me.'

Shauna's heart constricted. Jamie's tone said it all: the echoing sadness about his father and the bitterness about his mother told the whole story.

'My mother's not a bad woman,' he went on, toying with his plate. 'She's just very self-centred. And a teenage boy who's just lost his father needs attention.'

'You started to get into trouble to get her attention?' Shauna surmised. She understood his motives very well. The death of a parent leaves a child grasping for any and all attention . . . for any and all security. She recalled her desperate efforts to win her aunt's interest and love.

'At first,' he agreed. 'After a while, I didn't much care what I did. The only thing that mattered was music. I got involved with a local band when I was about seventeen. A couple of the members were older and into drugs and I went along. I was pretty messed up by the time I was arrested.' He swallowed down the remainder of his coffee. 'I still don't know how Michael found out I was in trouble, but he did. Because it was my first offence and the charge was only possession, I was able to get a suspended sentence and probation. After that, Michael got me into a rehabilitation programme. When I graduated, he talked my—our—mother into letting me come to live with him. We had some rough times, but he was always there for me. He was the one who helped put Tempest together when he saw I was serious about music.'

There was a long, reflective silence. What could she say after hearing a story like that?

'Are you finished?' The waitress materialised by their table. 'Anything more I can get you?'

For some inexplicable reason, this mundane question struck both of them as very funny. They began laughing. The waitress looked mystified and slightly affronted.

'Yeah, thanks, we're finished,' Jamie got out, grinning.

'Thank you,' Shauna echoed. 'May we have the bill?'

'My treat,' Jamie declared.

'No, I'll pay my share.'

'I'm paying,' he said flatly, but his brown eyes started to dance. 'I don't ask a woman to spend the weekend on the road with me and then not feed her.'

'Jamie!' Shauna blushed as the waitress handed him the bill and gave her an interested look before she hustled away with their dirty dishes.

'Yes, Shauna?' he enquired with feigned innocence.

'I think I'm taking back my acceptance of your apology.'

'No, you're not,' he returned easily. 'Hey, did Michael make you blush last night? When he came into the bedroom and woke you up, I mean.'

'That's none of your business,' she informed him stiffly, her cheeks blazing.

'Just curious.' He dropped several dollar bills on the table, then checked his watch. 'Look at the time!' he exclaimed. 'I've got to get my act together and get to rehearsal. Do you want to come along?'

It was the perfect opening to tell him about her

decision to leave, but, somehow, the words wouldn't come.

'I—I don't know,' she faltered. 'I have a few things I have to take care of . . .'

'Oh.' He looked disappointed as they made their way out of the coffee shop. 'Well, I understand how it is. You can come over later, maybe. If you want to, of course.'

'I'll have to see,' she temporised.

'OK. To tell the truth, it isn't going to be that interesting. We have to run through a couple of numbers and iron out a few technical kinks.'

'You were all terrific last night.'

'I know,' he said cheekily. 'But the boss is going to be in the audience tonight, so Tempest has to be perfect.' Leaning forward impulsively, he dropped a light kiss on her nose. 'Gotta run. See you later.'

When she'd come down for breakfast, Shauna had left her case at the front desk. Now, filled with a confusing sense of sadness, she walked over to retrieve it. She wondered how long she'd have to wait for a train back to New York City.

You're doing the right thing, she told herself. Leave now, before anything else happens. You know something else will happen if you don't.

What are you afraid of? another small voice within her asked.

'Excuse me—' She caught the attention of the prissy but polite-faced desk clerk.

'Yes?'

'I left my case here,' she said. 'It's brown, with an identification tag—'

'Oh, that was returned.' The clerk smiled helpfully, then glanced beyond her. Like an animal finely attuned to a stalker, Shauna felt a ripple of warning run through her.

'Returned?' she repeated.

'I had it sent back up to the suite.'

Even though, subconsciously, she had been braced to hear Michael's voice, she still stiffened with surprise.

She turned away from the desk and tilted her chin up slightly as she confronted him.

'I beg your pardon?' she asked coolly.

'I had it sent back up to the suite.' He was dressed in well-tailored black slacks and a cream cashmere turtle-neck. Over that he wore a black leather jacket—buttery soft, beautifully styled, and obviously expensive. His hands were thrust casually into the pockets of the jacket and his legs were braced, slightly apart, as though he was prepared to move, instantly, in any direction. He projected both polished sophistication and a street fighter's toughness. It was an unsettling combination.

'I don't believe you,' she said, wishing he wasn't standing so close.

'No? Then why don't you take this and check for yourself?' 'This' was a metal room key. He pressed it into her hand, his fingers briefly stroking her soft palm as he did so.

She glanced automatically at the plastic tag attached to the key and gave a small gasp of outrage as she saw it bore the room number of the suite where she—where they—had spent the previous night.

Shauna glared at him. 'If you think for one second that I am going to set foot in your hotel room again, Mr Sebastian, you are insane,' she said in a low, tight voice.

'Last night it was my room. Today it's yours—although SEE will still be paying the bill, of course.'

'What?' It came out louder than she intended and the clerk, who had been eavesdropping shamelessly, cleared his throat.

'Excuse me, Mr Sebastian,' he interrupted. 'Is there some problem?'

Michael gave him a brief smile. 'A small mix-up in accommodation,' he explained, taking a firm grip on Shauna's arm. 'We'll sort it out.' With that, he coolly marched her over to a relatively private section of the lobby.

'Let go!' Shauna hissed, trying to jerk away from him. He let go of her.

'Sit down,' he instructed succinctly.

For a moment, she considered throwing the key she was still holding back into his strong, arrogant face and stalking away, but she knew instinctively that such an act of defiance would look childish—to say nothing of quite possibly being dangerous. After a brief hesitation, she seated herself on the edge of one of the blue and cream upholstered chairs in the alcove furniture grouping he'd dragged her over to. She arranged her features into what she hoped was a suitably disdainful expression.

His mobile lips twitched as he took the chair nearest her. 'I see Miss Whitney is back,' he observed, his green eyes running over her assessingly.

'I have no idea what you're talking about,' she informed him huffily.

'Hair up.' To her dismay, he leaned forward and brushed his fingers lightly down the side of her head. 'Securely buttoned in.' He flicked the closed collar of her shirt. 'And all defences firmly in place.' He withdrew his hand. 'The only thing that's missing is your glasses.'

She was quivering inside. 'That's because you still have them,' she snapped, angry at her weakness.

'So I do,' he agreed amiably. 'And as long as I do, there's a chink in your Miss Whitney armour, isn't there, sweetheart? Those beautiful eyes of yours are too expressive, Shauna. They give you away every time.'

She experienced—but swiftly fought down—a spurt of pleasure at the passing compliment and the casually used endearment.

'Tell me,' she said evenly, meeting his bold, jade gaze, 'are my eyes giving away the fact that I think you are the rudest, most high-handed man I've ever met in my life?'

'That . . . and a few other things,' he replied lazily. 'But I'm not offended. I don't think you've met very many men in your life.'

She clenched her hands. 'Don't change the subject. I want—I want to know what you did with my suitcase.'

'I already told you what I did with it,' he answered in a reasonable tone. He seemed perfectly relaxed.

'You actually had it take up to your room?'

'*Your* room,' he corrected. 'I'm vacating the premises and doubling up with Jamie. Didn't he tell you that during your little tête-à-tête in the coffee shop?'

'How did you—' She stopped herself abruptly. She didn't want to know how he knew she and Jamie had been talking. Had he been lurking around somewhere in the restaurant watching—or even listening? Had he seen how she had drunk in the moving story of what he had done for his half-brother? 'Yes,' she answered shortly. 'Jamie said something about your moving in with him here at the hotel.'

'And did you say something to him about running away back to Manhattan? Was that affectionate peck on the nose he gave you meant to be a fond farewell kiss?' There was an acid edge to the enquiry.

'I am not running away,' she returned defensively. She wasn't going to talk about the kiss from Jamie. It had been nothing—and it was none of Michael's business. He was a fine one to bring up the subject of kissing!

'What would you call it?'

'Being sensible.'

'Playing it safe, you mean.'

'And what's wrong with that?' she demanded.

'What are you so afraid of?' he challenged, his green eyes pinning to her chair as he asked the same question she had addressed to herself earlier.

You! She wanted to blurt it out. I'm afraid of you. And I'm afraid of myself because of it.

'I'm not afraid,' she said quietly, looking down at her balled fists. She relaxed her hands, swallowing hard.

'Prove it,' came the trenchant response.

Her head came up. 'How?' The single syllable came out of her reluctantly because she could already see where he was manoeuvring her.

'Stay for the rest of the weekend.'

'I—can't.'

'You won't,' he countered.

'It's impossible, don't you see that? After what happened last night—' She gestured. 'And I answered the phone this morning when Carla Decker called, remember? It's going to be difficult enough as it is filling in for Dee without getting myself more involved than I already am in a situation that's bound to cause plenty of gossip.'

'And you think staying here another night would do that?'

'Don't you?'

He shook his head. 'No. Right now, as far as anyone is concerned, we were the victims of a simple mix-up. At most, it was an irritating inconvenience. But if you suddenly change your plans and go tearing back to New York, it will look a bit suspicious. Shrug last night off and people—if they should hear something about it— will shrug it off, too. React like a ravished hysteric and they'll start to speculate about what *really* happened.'

Shauna remained silent for a moment. Distasteful as it was to admit, Michael was making sense. 'What about Miss Decker?' she asked finally.

'Forget Carla. She won't say a word,' he replied curtly, closing off the subject.

She hesitated, worrying her lower lip with her even, white teeth. 'You honestly think I should stay?'

'Yes. Go to the concert tonight and go back to Manhattan tomorrow. And try to stop behaving as though I'm a depraved, would-be rapist with a highly contagious disease.'

'I don't behave—'

'A slight exaggeration,' he cut in smoothly. 'But your response to me is a bit unusual.'

'I haven't fallen under the notorious Sebastian spell, in other words?' she asked tartly.

'I suppose you could put it that way.'

'What about the way you've been behaving towards me?'

'Perhaps I've fallen under the notorious Whitney spell.'

Their eyes met and locked for a moment, her gaze questioning, his supplying no answers.

'I don't think so,' she said, shaking her head slowly as though trying to assimilate the pieces of a complicated puzzle. 'I don't think you're the type of man to fall under any woman's spell.' She caught her breath, not believing she'd actually said the words aloud.

His lips curved into a cynical smile. 'You're probably right,' he replied. 'I learned to distrust women very young. It makes a man less susceptible to spells. However . . . no one is completely immune.' He let this comment dangle enigmatically for several seconds before his manner changed, his charm coming to the fore.

'Shauna, I'm not proposing anything complicated or indecent. We've run into each other three times. Four, if you count that little episode with Carla in the elevator. None of those meetings has been a triumph in human relations. Even without the kind of gossip you're worried about, I don't think that's a track record that bodes well for our working together during the next two weeks. So, let's just spend a quiet day together. You get to know me. I get to know you.'

'Well . . .' She realised she was casting about for excuses to refuse. She wanted to spend the day with him . . . She wanted to get to know Michael Sebastian. But she was still afraid.

'Don't think about it, Miss Whitney. Just do it.' He extended his hand to her as he rose in a fluidly athletic movement.

She didn't make a conscious decision to take his hand. Impulse—ever present, always dangerous—compelled her to do so.

As she stood up, she tried not to think about what she might be getting herself into.

What she got herself into was a remarkably enjoyable day. Gradually—so gradually, in fact, that it seemed like the most natural thing in the world—she found herself succumbing to Michael Sebastian's attraction. While his manner was sometimes teasingly flirtatious, it had little of the dangerous mockery or the disturbingly sexual directness that had so disconcerted her on previous occasions.

He stayed by her side through everything: Tempest's rehearsal, a laughter-filled lunch with the road crew, and the concert that evening. He was flatteringly curious about her, and if some of his questions—particularly those about her time with her Aunt Margaret—were too perceptive for comfort, she still found herself wanting to give him the answers he was seeking. It felt curiously right to be talking with him. It also felt curiously right to have him lean close to whisper an explanation or a wry remark, or to have him drop his arm lightly over her shoulders as he guided her through the chaos backstage at the auditorium before the concert.

It was only when the concert was over and they returned to the hotel for the night that her earlier uneasiness returned. Shauna and Michael were in the lift alone, Jamie and the other band members having got off at their floor with a chorus of hearty good nights. Wordlessly, Michael thumbed the proper button.

'I thought you were rooming with Jamie,' she said after a moment, hoping her tone didn't betray her sudden resurgence of nervousness.

'I am,' he replied. 'But I have to get my things from the suite.'

'Oh.' She digested this. 'I—I repacked your bag for you and put it by the door,' she volunteered after a pause.

'Thank you. I'm surprised you didn't throw it out.'

'I did consider it,' she confessed with a laugh. She felt light-headed and oddly keyed-up.

The lift rose smoothly to the top floor. Stepping out, they walked to the suite in silence. Shauna unlocked the door, entering first. She quickly flipped on a light.

'There's your bag,' she said, pointing unnecessarily.

He nodded but made no move to pick it up. 'Do you want me to look around for you?' he asked, the gold in his eyes glinting. 'You can never tell what might be hiding in the bedroom.'

Shauna shook her head once. 'No . . . no, I don't think you need to do that,' she returned, restlessly reaching up and patting her hair.

She'd changed her clothes before the concert, unpinning her chignon and donning jeans, boots, and a softly cowled white sweater. Layered on top was an extra-large black T-shirt, a present from the band. Emblazoned across the front in bold silver stencilling was the legend 'TEMPEST NATIONAL TOUR'.

Despite the bagginess of the garment, the movement of her breasts was evident as she lifted her arm. The delicate fullness drew Michael's eyes. His gaze lingered there for a few seconds before returning to her face.

'Don't be afraid, Shauna,' he said softly. So softly that she thought she might be imagining the words.

Whether she came to him or he to her—or whether they simply met half-way—she was never certain. All she remembered afterwards was that one moment she had known he was about to kiss her and the next moment he was doing so.

His mouth was teasing yet tender as it moved over hers, tasting her lips with deliberate gentleness. He made no effort to deepen his slow, sensual caress until she began to open to him with shy sweetness.

With leisurely expertise he explored her, drinking in her secrets and savouring the flavour of her flowering response. One of his hands moved down her back, fingers stroking the indentation of her spine through her clothes, finally coming to rest just below her waist. The other hand slipped around her neck, cupping the back of her head.

Shauna had been kissed before, but never this thoroughly, and never by a man as confidently male as Michael Sebastian. In some elemental way, his confidence gave her the courage to put aside—for the moment at least—her own insecurities and inhibitions. Instinctively, she parted her lips, inviting further intimacies. Her palms slid up his chest, learning its hard-muscled strength through the luxuriously fine knit of his sweater.

She was, in a way, testing herself as a woman—finding the keys to her long locked-up emotions. Michael allowed her to make her discoveries at her own speed . . . accepting, guiding, but never forcing the pace.

He was the one who pulled back at the point where their embrace began to arouse more hungers than it satisfied. Only the look in his eyes—a look Shauna was too bemused to interpret—betrayed how much of an effort he was expending in order to put her away from him with such firm gentleness.

'I said we should get to know each other today,' he said huskily. 'I think we've gone about far enough.'

'You do?' Shauna didn't know what she was feeling. She only knew she had never been so aware of her body and its sensations. She had never felt so utterly alive . . . and so totally unprepared.

'Yes, I do.' He stepped back and picked up his bag, watching her intently. She stared back at him, her fair skin softly rosy with a flush of arousal and her wide hazel eyes luminously, innocently eager.

She didn't want him to leave. But if he didn't leave . . .

Far enough, he had said. She wondered, dazedly, if he had any idea how far that was for her. She raised one hand and touched her lips delicately. Too far.

'Good night, Michael,' she said.

He nodded, accepting and understanding the situation better than she did herself. Without speaking, he turned, opened the door with a jerk and walked out. There was a click as he shut the door behind him. The sound was like a punctuation mark at the end of a sentence. A period.

Not really seeing anything, Shauna walked to the door, touching its slick painted surface with newly sensitised fingertips. She started, her heart jolted into her throat, when she heard Michael's voice from the other side.

'Put the chain lock on, Shauna,' he instructed.

She did so.

'And the bolt.'

She obeyed him again, her fingers not quite steady.

'Good night.' The thick pile of the hall carpeting swallowed up the sound of his receding footsteps.

Shauna leaned her head against the door. She felt stripped of her long-standing defences, with her nerve endings quivering.

She stayed that way, trembling, for a long time.

CHAPTER SIX

THE events of the weekend were very much on Shauna's mind as she reluctantly but resolutely reported for work on Monday.

A man kissed you, nothing else, she told herself fiercely as she waited for the lift in the lobby of the SEE building. All right, he kissed you twice—three times! But it didn't mean anything to him. And it shouldn't mean anything to you, either!

Because she'd made it a point to arrive at the office early, she had the lift to herself on the way up. She slipped off her coat, making a minute adjustment in the fall of the moss green, burgundy, and cream paisley dress she was wearing. A co-ordinating Chanel-style cardigan jacket completed the outfit.

But *why* had he kissed her that third time?

She smoothed her palm slowly down the length of her hair as the lift glided to a stop. She hadn't done her hair up into its customary chignon this morning. Instead, she'd swept the front off her forehead and clipped it in place with a barrette. The remainder of it cascaded over her shoulders in soft chestnut waves.

He was trying to charm you, she thought. It will be different when you're working with him. You'll see him for what he really is.

The reception area was done in cool shades of grey and furnished in leather, glittering chrome and smoked glass. The polished sleekness of the walls was punctuated by dozens of framed album covers and clusters of award plaques.

The colour scheme and the potently contemporary aura carried over into the area where she would be working. It was not an atmosphere Shauna found particularly comfortable, but she decided it would make it easier for her to maintain a realistic, businesslike attitude.

It wasn't until she sat down, mentally gearing herself for the day ahead, that she saw a small bouquet of flowers sitting in a vase on the corner of the desk. The blossoms—a cluster of daisies, a handful of white chrysanthemums, and a single red rosebud—were casually arranged. Her features softening in puzzled delight, Shauna leaned forward to sniff the delicate perfume of the rose. She recognised the bouquet as the sort of thing sold by street vendors. It was not what she'd expected to find here.

'I took a chance that you weren't allergic to flowers,' a velvet soft male voice said.

Shauna started, hot colour flooding up into her cheeks. She turned. 'Michael!' she gasped. 'I mean, Mr Sebastian—'

'You mean Michael, Shauna,' he said tolerantly. He'd been lounging against the frame of the door to his office, watching her through half-lidded eyes. He straightened now, his tall, lean body moving with deceptively lazy grace.

Shauna stiffened unwittingly, feeling as though the size of the room had shrunk by about fifty per cent.

The casual clothes she was accustomed to seeing him wear were nowhere in sight this Monday. Today, he was clad in an impeccably styled charcoal grey suit, a white silk shirt, and a discreetly patterned tie. The obviously custom-tailored fit of his jacket enhanced his natural masculine elegance and also hinted at the muscular power of his body. A strand of dark hair had fallen over his brow. Shauna watched, mesmerised, as he brushed it back in a careless gesture.

'M-Michael,' she stammered out. Forcing herself to look away from him, she glanced down at her hands. They were clenched, white-knuckled and trembling, on the top of the desk. She moved them down into her lap. 'I—You—' She took a deep breath, willing herself back into control. 'Thank you for the flowers,' she said finally.

A fraction of a second later, she glanced up at him.

He smiled. 'You're welcome. You're also early.' There was a faint enquiry in the last observation. Shauna felt his green gaze rove over her, ticking off each detail of her appearance.

'I wanted to familiarise myself with a few things before the day actually got started,' she explained. 'Dee went over your calendar and most of the basics last week before she left, but I thought I'd refresh my memory.' Dee had been very helpful and friendly, but she had, indeed, been caught up in what Michael had described as a 'pre-honeymoon haze'. Shauna suspected there had been some things left out of her briefing, and she wanted to discover what they were before the work day got underway.

Michael nodded. 'Good idea. Did she remember to leave you her VIP list?'

'Yes.'

'Good. If it has her usual dose of editorialising, I suggest you keep it locked up in a safe place.'

Shauna laughed. He knew his secretary well. Dee had entrusted her with a list of people who were to be given kid-glove treatment. Next to a number of names she had written in comments—some complimentary, some critical, and most scathingly funny. Carla Decker's name was near the top of the list, followed by several asterisks, exclamation marks, and the notation 'Immediate Access—any time, any place'.

'Actually, I'm planning to burn it at the end of the two weeks,' she told him.

'Smart lady.'

There was a brief break in the conversation. Again, Shauna felt the room grow smaller.

'Are you—do you normally arrive this early?' she asked eventually. Surreptitiously, she pressed her hands against the fabric of her dress. Her palms were damp.

'I had trouble sleeping,' he replied laconically. He crossed over to a grey metal filing cabinet on the opposite side of the room and pulled open the top drawer.

'Oh.' It was a perfectly unexceptional explanation. Why did she find herself conjuring up all kinds of disturbing images in response to it? She shook her head. 'Is there—Is there something I can do for you?'

He extracted a folder and slid the drawer shut. 'Coffee,' he replied, leafing through the papers in the file. 'You can make some.' He frowned over something he was reading. 'After you've done that, bring your pad into my office. I've got a backlog of correspondence to catch up on.'

She rose gracefully. Making coffee would give her enough time to get a good steady grip on herself. 'How do you take your coffee?' she asked.

'Black with sugar.' His mouth quirked suddenly as he looked over at her, the gold gleaming in his narrowed eyes. 'Hot and sweet, Miss Whitney.'

Professionally, Michael Sebastian led a pressure-cooker existence, and Shauna was plunged right into the middle of it with him. Within an hour of her arrival, she was inundated by what seemed to be a ceaseless stream of instructions from Michael and an endless variety of calls and visitors for him.

That she could handle the work, and handle it well, both surprised and delighted her. She'd absorbed more than she'd realised working in the Legal Department. Her common sense got her through the unfamiliar territory.

She found herself studying Michael, trying to anticipate his needs and orders, looking for clues about the way his mercurial mind was working. He was not an easy man to decipher. Tough, ambitious businessman . . . talented musician . . . practised and practising charmer —there was something of the chameleon about him. And for all his directness and varied moods, he revealed very little about his inner thoughts and feelings. Michael guarded himself very well.

Any hopes she'd had that seeing him at close quarters would reawaken her initial hostilities towards him quickly vanished. By the time she'd been in the job three days, she'd come to respect his energy, his judgment, and his restless desire to achieve and create.

His attitude towards her was difficult to gauge. While they seemed to mesh well professionally, she was uneasily aware of an unspoken undercurrent at the personal level. There were times when Shauna had the feeling Michael was testing her and probing her defences. He had a habit of asking her questions about her past at the most unpredictable moments. He also had an unnerving way of looking at her, his green eyes waiting and watchful.

Still, it was nothing she could quite put her finger on. And each time she was about to challenge him on his behaviour, his manner would change, leaving her to wonder if she'd been imagining things.

Late in the afternoon on Wednesday of her first week substituting for Dee, Michael informed Shauna he wanted her to accompany him to a Greenwich Village club that evening to hear a musician who had been recommended as a possible client for SEE. There was something faintly aggressive about the way he extended the invitation; although he phrased it as a request, Shauna sensed Michael was not about to take no for an answer.

'This is part of the business,' Michael said, seeing her instinctive hesitation. Part of her wanted to accept eagerly. Another part, the part that had controlled her behaviour for so long, warned she needed to be cautious. 'I told you before you agreed to work for me that the job meant long hours. You said that wasn't a problem.'

'Well—'

'Do you have a date?'

'I—'

'Do you, Shauna?' His green eyes had gone emerald as he leaned forward on her desk. The question was sharp, almost angry.

Shauna's brows came together. 'N-no, I don't have a

date,' she replied, nettled by his tone.

'Then there's no problem about your coming with me.'

You're the only problem, she thought, forcing herself to look away from his compelling and far too perceptive gaze. She fiddled briefly with a stack of correspondence she had been typing up when he'd come into her work area.

'I'm not sure I'm dressed properly,' she said finally, glancing down at herself. She was wearing a demure, grey flannel shirt-waister dress with crisp white collar and cuffs. A silky, wine paisley neck scarf softened the garment's starkness a bit. Her long hair was neatly coiled into a knot at the nape of her neck and small pearl earrings nestled in the lobes of her ears.

'You're dressed too properly for my taste,' Michael replied. He said it so mildly that the implication of the comment did not strike Shauna for several seconds. When it did, she looked up at him, her expression both apprehensive and questioning. His face was composed, but his eyes held that disconcerting look of assessment once again.

'I don't think—' she began.

'If you're uncomfortable with what you're wearing, go home and change.'

'Now?'

He nodded.

'But—it's not quitting time yet. I can't leave early.'

'Why not? Afraid you're going to get in trouble with the boss?' His tone was gently mocking.

'Mr Sebastian—' Instinctively, she sought refuge in formality.

'Miss Whitney,' he countered silkily, reaching across the desk and brushing a silencing finger over her lips. 'Go home—now,' he instructed. 'Change your clothes. I'll pick you up at seven. We'll get something to eat before the show.'

'That's not necessary,' she protested.

'Probably not,' he agreed, shrugging. 'But it's what I

want, and it's what you're going to do. You've got to stop saying "no" to me all the time, Shauna.'

The slow, deliberately sensual smile that accompanied the last sentence made her colour hotly. Yet there was an odd pensiveness lurking in the depths of his eyes as he spoke. It hinted at a totally unexpected vulnerability in a man whose instinct for emotional self-preservation was ruthlessly and relentlessly evident.

'I—Do you know where I live?' she faltered.

'I had your personal folder pulled.'

'Oh.' It was a perfectly reasonable and understandable thing for him to have done. Yet the idea of it disturbed her. Don't be an idiot, she berated herself. He knows more about you from reading your poetry than a personnel folder could ever tell—

'Shauna?'

The concerned intensity in his voice told her how much of her internal turmoil must be showing on her face. She struggled to get herself under control, calling on the bitterly unhappy lessons she'd learned under Aunt Margaret's stern tutelage.

'I—Nothing,' she got out. 'I—I'll see you at my apartment at seven, then. Thank you.'

She knew, without looking at him, that Michael was on the verge of pressing her, of probing her yet again with questions. Something, however, made him back off.

'At seven,' he repeated. Pivoting on his heel, he walked back into his office and shut the door.

Shauna found herself unusually indecisive when it came to making up her mind about what to wear that evening. She sorted through her limited wardrobe three or four times, growing increasingly dissatisfied with the demurely practical garments that filled her small cupboard.

Michael's comment about the extreme propriety of her office attire had rankled. It reminded her—as if she needed any reminding!—of just how self-consciously prim she must seem compared with the sophisticated, free-wheeling women he was used to. She wished she had just *one* outfit . . .

At the same time, however, she wasn't about to go changing herself around to please Michael Sebastian! And she certainly didn't want him to think she was regarding this evening as anything other than an extension of her duties as his assistant.

And yet . . .

Finally, with the clock showing just fifteen minutes before seven, she settled on a country-style brown corduroy skirt and an écru cotton blouse with a touch of crocheted lace at the collar and cuffs. Over this she added a sleeveless knitted vest in varying tones of brown, tan, and rust. At the last second, acting purely on impulse, she freed her hair from its neat coil at the nape of her neck and brushed it loose over her slender shoulders.

Michael was very prompt. He'd also found time to change, replacing a business suit with jeans and a navy turtle-neck sweater and trading his expensive, ultra-executive tan raincoat for a battered pea-jacket of obviously ancient vintage. It made him seem younger and more approachable in a way. It also emphasised the street-wise sensuality that lurked behind his professional polish.

'Come in,' Shauna invited politely.

'Thanks,' Michael replied. 'I'm glad to see you're not completely cavalier when it comes to using locks,' he commented blandly, nodding at the collection of bolts and chains on her door.

'I—Oh.' She silently damned the betraying rush of hot blood that flooded up into her cheeks as she realised what he was referring to. 'No . . . I'm not usually careless about such things,' she said, wishing she didn't remember in such vivid detail what had happened the one and only time she had been careless.

'Good.' He nodded and looked around him with undisguised interest.

Shauna's apartment wasn't very large. The furniture she had—and her budget hadn't allowed for many major purchases—was mostly second-hand. Three sets of floor-to-ceiling shelves crammed with books betrayed where most of her money went. The wall opposite the shelves was decorated with a collection of inexpensive posters. Several of them were reproductions of famous Impressionist masterpieces. Shauna found their serene and airy beauty deeply appealing.

'Not exactly what you expected?' she asked Michael, recalling the question he had thrown at her that day in his elegant apartment. There was something unnervingly intent about the way he was studying the room.

'On the contrary,' he returned, running a hand through his hair. His voice was softly satisfied.

Shauna shifted awkwardly, trying not to dwell on the possible implications of this response. 'It's not much,' she said. 'Of course, I'm lucky to have any place at all, given the housing situation in New York. So, I really can't complain. But—but there are moments when I wish I had a view.' She made the admission with a trace of wistfulness, gesturing towards the room's two small windows. Both were effectively blocked by the crisscross of a metal fire escape landing.

'The view's just fine from where I'm standing.'

His tone was so casual that it took her a moment to register that he wasn't talking about what he could—or couldn't—see from her apartment windows. She stared at him, her eyes wide and uncertain.

'That was a compliment, Miss Whitney,' he told her gently, his mouth curving into a smile that held equal parts of friendliness and flirtation. The warmth of his green gaze as he met her questioning stare was unshadowed and inviting.

'I—Thank you.' Her heart gave a strange flutter as she returned his smile with shy pleasure.

'You're welcome. You're also going to have to get used to my appreciating the way you look.'

Her smile vanished. 'Get used—?' she began in a taut little voice.

'Mmmm . . .' He nodded pensively, glancing around the room again. 'You know, this is a far cry from the first place I had when I came to New York . . . a very far cry.' He gave a dry laugh. 'Of course, I spent about six months crashing wherever I could before I could afford to pay any rent at all. When I finally saved up a few dollars, I moved into what can charitably be described as a broom closet in the basement of a tenement. Luckily for me, the landlord didn't give a damn about the fact that I was under age. As long as I paid him on time and in full, he really didn't care one way or the other what the date on my birth certificate was.'

The sudden shift of subject caught Shauna off guard. So did the unexpected sharing of what was plainly a very private memory. There was no bitterness in the way Michael spoke, no bid for sympathy. If anything, he seemed amused . . . as though he took ironic pride in reflecting on how far he had come from where he had started.

But how hard it must have been for a teenage boy on his own! And how much the journey must have cost him!

'You came to Manhattan after leaving the Cor—' The question came out of its own volition. Shauna tried to bite it back when she realised how personal it was.

Michael's brows went up. 'I came here after I ran away from the Cord family out in Chicago, yes,' he confirmed with precision. He paused for a moment, his expression assessing. 'Let me guess: Jamie told you. When? Over breakfast in Hartford?'

'He—We talked about a number of things that morning,' Shauna admitted hesitantly, trying to get a fix on his reaction and wishing he weren't quite so adept at masking his feelings. Was Michael angry at Jamie for talking to her? Did he resent her knowing some of the details of his early life? Did he think she would find those details shocking or shameful?

Shauna dismissed this last possibility almost before

the idea was fully formed. Why should Michael
Sebastian care what she thought? He was a man who
went his own way, independent and uncaring of other
people's opinions. The notion that her reaction to anything would make the slightest bit of difference to him
was . . . ridiculous.

'Jamie did tell me that you lived with his family for a
year after your father died,' she went on slowly, feeling
as though she might be tiptoeing into an emotional
minefield. 'He said you l-left very suddenly and he didn't
know what had happened to you until "You Made Me
What I Am" was released.' She worried her lower lip
with her teeth for a moment, uncertain of whether or not
she should continue. Finally, she decided Michael had
a right to know how much Jamie had revealed. 'Jamie
told me how you helped him when he was in . . . in
trouble.'

'That's not a story my brother usually offers for public
consumption,' he observed quietly.

'I—I won't say anything about it to anyone,' Shauna
reassured him quickly, thinking he was concerned about
gossip.

An odd smile tugged at the corner of his mouth.
Before she realised what he meant to do, he'd lifted one
hand and very gently brushed a finger down the curve of
cheek. The light, fleeting touch made her catch her
breath.

'I know you won't,' he returned. 'You're a lady who's
very good at keeping secrets, aren't you? But don't
make too much out of the role I played in Jamie's
troubles. He was the one who did the hard part.'

'You were there when he needed you.'

'Yes . . . well, I owed him that. Jamie was the best
thing I got out of that year with the Cords. Besides, I
know what it's like to be in over your head.'

Their eyes locked and held for a long moment. Shauna
was conscious of the almost painful beating of her heart
. . . the throbbing of her pulse. The bond of communication stretching between them was a tangible thing.

Part of her shrank away from the pull of it; another part ached to be drawn in.

Michael broke the spell without warning, his green eyes suddenly shuttered. He glanced down at his watch in an abrupt gesture. 'We'd better get going,' he said tersely. 'We don't want to be late.'

The club he took her to was located in a squatty, two-storey stone building. It had been in the same spot for years, Michael told her as they travelled downtown by taxi, attracting music lovers long before Greenwich Village developed an international reputation as a haven for Bohemian artists and free thinkers.

'Watch your step,' he warned as he helped her out of the cab once they arrived.

'Thank you,' she said gratefully, using his arm to steady herself. The weather of the past two days had been punctuated by intermittent snow flurries and freezing drizzle. The combination had left pavements hazardously coated with ice.

Even without the revealing light of day to judge by, Shauna could tell that the front of the club wasn't very prepossessing. It was about as welcoming as an old warehouse, in fact—a far cry from the trendy, ultra-fashionable places she assumed Michael normally frequented. The building's only distinguished feature was an ornate neon sign that bluntly declared: 'This is the Place'.

'It's better inside,' Michael grinned, his white teeth flashing briefly in the glow of a nearby street lamp. He slipped a casual arm around Shauna's waist and escorted her inside.

The interior was better. Although decorated in a haphazard jumble of styles, it had a comfortable, unpretentious atmosphere. A huge wooden bar surrounded by clusters of patrons dominated one side of the room. The white-washed brick walls were covered with old newspaper clippings, theatrical posters, and framed black and white photographs. Tables of various sizes and shapes were arranged around the dark, hardwood floor in no apparent pattern. A stairway marked with an arrow reading 'Music This Way' led to the second storey.

'Do you come here often?' Shauna asked curiously after they had been seated at a table and had their orders taken. Something about the treatment they were being accorded hinted that Michael Sebastian was a familiar —and favoured—customer.

Michael smiled. 'I used to work here.'

'You did?'

'I washed dishes.'

'Washed dishes!'

He nodded. 'That's right. A seventeen-year-old kid whose only skills are playing the guitar and writing songs isn't very employable, you know. I was damn lucky to land a job here. Of course, the pay was terrible, but I got a free meal from the kitchen every night I worked. And, after a while, I started to meet people.' He looked around, his expression reflective. 'This place may not look very chic but, sooner or later, everybody who's anybody in the music business comes drifting through.'

'I—I don't imagine you stayed a dish washer very long.'

'Long enough. Eventually, I started making connections . . . started to learn how things work. I was a very quick student.' There was an edge of self-mockery to the last sentence. 'I did pick-up gigs in some of the sleaziest places imaginable. I played back-up in studio sessions for people nobody's ever heard of. And I auditioned my songs for anybody who'd listen to them. Eventually, it paid off.'

'You stopped performing when your songs started to sell, didn't you?' It was something she'd wondered about. Her mind flashed back to the scene in his apartment . . . to the song he'd sung and the way he'd sung it. With his talent, dark good looks, and compelling sexual charisma, she was certain Michael Sebastian could have easily become a star—a pop idol. Yet he had chosen to avoid that path. Why?

'I wanted to be in control of my life—and my work,' he said, answering her unspoken question. 'I didn't want to be somebody else's commodity, which is what you've got to let yourself be turned into if you're going to succeed as a performer.' He paused, seeming to choose his words with care. When he spoke, his voice had taken on a chilling, crystalline precision. 'Besides, by the time I scored with "You Made Me What I Am", I'd had my fill of people who thought that if I was willing to sell my music in public, I'd be willing to sell myself in private as well. I don't . . . perform on demand.'

Shauna caught her breath. Instinct told her that she had just been given a key piece to the complicated puzzle that made up Michael Sebastian's personality. But what had prompted such a revelation? Was he testing her in some way? Trying to warn her off? Could it be, in some odd way, a bid for her understanding?

Or, perhaps, he found some perverse amusement in deliberately underscoring the gulf between his experience and her lack of it.

She was so caught up in this jumble of speculation that she didn't realise their waiter had returned until he began serving their dinner. His appearance gave her a chance to recover herself, and for this she was grateful. Her uncertainties about Michael's motives this evening made her feel very vulnerable.

'Thank you very much,' she murmured to the waiter. She'd ordered a chicken and mushroom casserole described as a specialty of the house. The dish gave off a rich, savoury fragrance.

'At a loss for words, Miss Whitney?' Michael asked softly after the waiter moved away.

She looked at him, her eyes clouded with wary questioning. While his enquiry had a hint of challenge in it, his expression was surprisingly gentle. 'What—what do you want me to say?'

His mobile lips twisted. He took a deep breath, expelling it slowly. 'I don't know,' he said finally. He held her gaze for a long moment before dropping his eyes to his own entrée of rare steak and salad. He picked up his fork, his strong musician's fingers circling the utensil almost caressingly. 'I really don't know.'

'Michael—'

He gave a small shake of his head. 'Eat,' he instructed quietly.

Shauna felt the stirring of an alien emotion deep within her. Whatever his reasons, Michael had opened the door of his life to her. Now he was shutting it again. Something in Shauna's heart cried out in silent protest against that. She wanted to do . . . to say . . . something.

But she was restrained by the walls and locked doors of her own upbringing. With the obedience of a child, she began to eat.

Michael's ruthless exercise of charm and her own innate courtesy got them through the meal without further incident. In fact, by the time they adjourned to the second storey of the club to hear the evening's performance, they were embroiled in a friendly—if resolutely impersonal—discussion of popular music. Although Michael, with his experience and expertise, could have dominated the exchange, he did not. Instead, he drew Shauna out with subtle skill, overcoming her instinctive reticence with a flattering show of interest in her opinions.

The artist they had come to hear proved to be a pianist-singer in his mid-twenties with a flair for jazzy improvisation. Although most of his repertoire consisted of well-known contemporary hits—including a few songs written by Michael Sebastian—he had a knack for presenting the words and music with a fresh style. Glancing over at Michael during the performer's ruefully regretful version of 'You Made Me What I Am', Shauna saw him give a barely perceptible nod of approval.

'You thought he was good, didn't you?' Shauna asked as they left the club about twenty minutes later. She shivered a little as the cold night air struck her and thrust her hands into the pockets of her camel wrap coat.

'Good with the potential of getting much better,' he replied, glancing assessingly up and down the side street where the club was located. 'We'd better walk over a few blocks,' he said. 'We'll never get a cab here. You won't freeze up on me, will you, sweetheart?'

The smile that accompanied this question seemed nicely calculated to raise her temperature by at least ten degrees. Shauna shook her head quickly. 'No. I'll be fine.'

They walked about a half-block in silence. 'What did you think of him?' Michael enquired. The question came out in a silvery cloud of vapour.

'I enjoyed the performance. Even though there weren't any original songs, he seemed to have—oh, I don't know exactly—his own style. The trouble with so much of the music today is that it all seems alike. But tonight—this didn't sound like anybody else.' She made a little face at the inadequacy of her description.

'Most of the demo tapes SEE gets are derivative,' Michael agreed. 'If someone creative comes up with a new, successful sound, everybody else in the business runs out and copies it. There are moments when I feel like I'm afflicted with a permanent case of professional *déjà vu*.' The look he gave her was full of a sudden conspiratorial amusement. An errant gust of wind ruffled his thick, dark hair, sending a lock of it curling boyishly down on to his forehead. 'That's why, when I find an original talent, I go out of my way to see it gets properly developed—no matter how much resistance I run into from the person who possesses the talent.'

Momentarily mesmerised by his potent appeal and caught up in the crazy urge to brush his hair back into place, Shauna nearly missed the edged emphasis of his words. When their underlying meaning penetrated, she halted in mid-stride, turning on him.

'Are you—Do you mean my poetry?' she asked.

One dark brow quirked upward in affirmation. 'Could be,' he replied with infuriating mildness. 'Although you seem equally resistant to exercising your other talents as well.'

'My other—' She stopped, searching his face for a moment before abruptly deciding she didn't want to pursue that last remark. 'The answer is no,' she said flatly.

'"No" to your poetry or "no" to your other talents?'

'I don't have any—No! Just *no*.' She looked down at the pavement blindly for a second or so, the silken length of her hair cascading forward, screening her expression. It still partially veiled her face when she glanced back up at him. 'I've already told you that.'

'So you have.'

'Then why don't you accept it?'

'Because you're very good,' he told her simply. 'And because—one way or another—I always get what I want.'

'Not this time.'

'Ah, but Miss Whitney, you don't know what I want.'

Reaching forward, he brushed at the heavy curtain of her hair. At the first leather-gloved touch of his fingers, Shauna jerked her head back like a frightened fawn. Trembling for reasons that had nothing to do with the cold, she took a sudden step away from him.

The move was too sudden, given the slick condition of the pavement. Gasping, she felt one heel skid on a patch of ice. In a desperate bid to save herself from falling, she overbalanced forward and stumbled into the unyielding hardness of Michael's body.

Even with the separating layers of winter clothing, Shauna was aware of the warmth and strength of him. The subtle, spicy scent of his aftershave—as well as the more basic male muskiness of his skin—filled her nostrils. His arms closed around her body, steadying and staying in the same movement.

The sensation of security was frightening in its seductiveness. Shauna turned her face up to look at him, her eyes huge in her pale, delicately featured face.

He was a heartbeat away from kissing her. The

devouring heat of his emerald gaze betrayed his intention with uninhibited clarity. What Michael Sebastian
wanted, Michael Sebastian got.

And what about what *she* wanted? Instinct—and a
sudden need—brought her lashes fluttering closed. Her
soft, waiting lips parted slightly.

But then, to her bewilderment, he let her go. With a
gentleness that made it an act of tenderness rather than
rejection, he released her.

'No.'

She stared up at him. 'Michael?' she had the strangest
sense he wasn't saying no to her . . . but to himself.

He shook his head. 'Some women's eyes you can get
lost in,' he went on softly. 'With yours—a man could
find himself, Shauna.'

'I—I don't understand.'

He muttered something under his breath then shoved
his hands deep into the pockets of his pea-jacket. The
tension in his body was obvious. His features coalesced
into a paganly handsome but stony mask.

'Let's get you home,' he said. 'Now, while I can still let
you go.'

CHAPTER SEVEN

'As efficient as ever, Miss Whitney,' Michael said pleasantly late the next morning as he casually dropped a sheaf of neatly typed letters on her desk. Each sheet of the expensive white stationery bore the vivid imprint of SEE's corporate letter-head and the bold scrawl of his signature.

'Thank you,' she returned, straightening the papers with careful precision. She glanced up at him for a moment, the flickering quicksilver in the depths of her hazel eyes at odds with the controlled tranquillity of her expression.

She'd come into the office not knowing what to expect. The previous night's combination of unanticipated intimacy and unexplained withdrawal had left her shaken.

She still didn't understand what had happened . . . and she wasn't at all certain she wanted to. Understanding would only draw her more deeply into something she already knew was dangerous.

Dangerous. It was an apt—although understated—description of Michael Sebastian as far as she was concerned. He was like an exotic, addictive drug. She could feel him in her bloodstream already, holding her in thrall with his music and his mystery. The more she knew of him, the more she wanted to learn. And the more she learned . . .

'Shauna?'

She started. 'Sorry,' she murmured, biting her lower lip.

She couldn't quarrel with his manner so far this morning. He'd been polite—even charming—to her. There hadn't been so much as a word, a look, or a gesture, she could point to or question.

Yet she bitterly resented every second of it. He was treating her like a stranger—an *enemy*.

Still, underneath the assured urbanity, the executive polish, she could detect the controlled, stony mask he had assumed the night before as he set her away from him. He was feeling something; something he felt impelled to hide.

What? she asked herself. And why?

She made a deliberate show of consulting the appointment calendar on her desk. Michael was standing motionless, watching her. She would be the impeccable, unapproachable secretary to his aloof employer. Her hard-won poise—and innate pride—would get her through this.

'You have a lunch at The Four Seasons in thirty minutes,' she informed him.

He nodded, running his hand through his hair. 'I know. It's likely to run long, so call Emmett Barkley and tell him to handle the afternoon meeting without me.'

'All right.' Her voice was mechanical.

'Did you manage to track down Kelso—the audio engineer I asked you to find?'

She handed him a slip of paper with an address and telephone number. It had taken a considerable amount of diplomacy and some ingenious detective work—to say nothing of three dozen calls—to locate the man, but she'd done it.

'He's willing to meet with you privately at four this afternoon to demonstrate his invention,' she said. 'Since your schedule looked clear—'

'Terrific.' He cut her off, scanning the paper. 'I definitely won't be back for the rest of the day, then. If the rumours about Kelso's new digital system are even half-way accurate, I want SEE to get in on the ground floor.' He shot her an assessing look. 'Did you have trouble finding him? He's got a reputation for being elusive.'

'No problem.'

'Good.' He seemed to be ticking down some kind of

mental list. 'About the meeting with Carla Decker's agent—'

'I've already taken care of that.'

'I see.' For the first time since they'd said their polite-voiced farewells the night before, his tone took on some colour. There was a metallic glint in his eyes. It was impossible to tell whether it was sparked by amusement or irritation. 'The demographics breakdown from Sales?' he enquired silkily.

With a deliberateness bordering on rudeness, Shauna flipped through the pages of her stenographic pad.

'It will be on your desk by noon tomorrow,' she reported. 'Just as you wanted.' Knowing it was an unwise thing to do, but taking a perverse satisfaction in doing so anyway, she gave him a small, insincere smile then reached for a pen.

With swift, jungle-cat grace, he leaned across the desk, trapping her hand in a decisive moment. 'And what I want, I get—is that it?' he challenged.

Shauna sucked in her breath, trying to ignore the warm, firm press of his palm over her fingers. There was nothing she could do about the sudden hammering of her pulse. She lifted her chin with uncharacteristic reck-lessness.

'I suppose that depends on what you want, Mr Sebastian,' she returned with a steadiness she was far from feeling.

'I suppose it does,' he agreed. His thumb stroked her slender wrist in a delicate circular movement, emphasis-ing and savouring the tender fragility of bone and flesh. There was a testing—and a temptation—in the contact. 'Aren't you going to ask me what I want, Miss Whitney?'

She shook her head in a gesture of denial as hot colour flooded up into her cheeks. *I know what you want* . . .

He released her hand, tilting his head slightly to one side. The slow, faintly sardonic curving of his sensual mouth told her he'd seen through her efforts to provoke him and accurately divined her unspoken response to his question.

'Try reading your poetry, Shauna,' he suggested softly
. . . and was gone.

Shauna immersed herself in her job for the rest of the
day, grateful for the distracting press of business. Yet,
just below the level of conscious thought, she was nag-
gingly aware of how empty the office seemed. It was an
awareness that did nothing for her peace of mind.

She tried to shape some of her restless, confused
feelings into a poem that night. After a half-dozen false
starts—each less satisfactory than the one before it
—she gave up. For once, there was no relief to be found
in spilling out her emotions on paper.

She slept badly and, in the first few minutes after being
awakened by her alarm, actually contemplated calling in
sick. Her innate distaste for such a cowardly deception
—plus the conviction that Michael Sebastian would see
through it—prevented her from doing so.

She hadn't counted on there being a breakdown on
the subway line she travelled. Some mysterious malfunc-
tion left her and scores of other impatient passengers
stranded underground for nearly an hour.

Michael was standing by her desk, on the phone, when
she finally arrived at the office. Her cheeks were pink
with cold and the exertion of a four-block dash from the
subway station.

'. . . there's nothing to discuss, Carla,' Michael was
saying. 'I've made the decision, babe. That's it. Goodbye.' He dropped the phone back into its cradle, making
no effort to disguise his temper. 'Where the hell have
you been?' he demanded of Shauna.

'I—I'm sorry I'm late,' she apologised, struggling to
catch her breath. She put down her bag and pulled off
her leather gloves. He had a right to be angry with her,
she acknowledged. In an odd way, she found the honest
display of emotion preferable to the aloofness of the day
before.

'Do you have any idea what I've been—'

'The subway broke down,' she hastened to explain,

tugging at the knot in the belt of her wrap coat. 'I'm very sorry.'

'The *subway*?' To her astonishment, his temper vanished. He relaxed visibly. 'Take it easy,' he instructed reassuringly, seeing how shaky she was. 'I'm not going to—' He broke off as the phone shrilled. He answered it before she even reacted to the sound.

Shauna stared at him, unable to hide her bewilderment at this mercurial shift of mood.

'No, Emmett, everything's fine,' Michael said pleasantly, giving her an unexpectedly warm smile. 'She just walked in. There was some problem with the subway. What? Of course—Don't worry about her. Incidentally, you may be getting an angry call from Carla's lawyer. Tell him the arrangement stands . . . Thanks.'

'You called Mr Barkley because I was late?' Shauna asked in a shocked voice as he hung up the phone. She knew that SEE's chief legal counsel put an old-fashioned premium on punctuality. No doubt her tardiness would be held against her.

Michael shook his head. 'No. I called him because I was worried when you didn't come in on time. You're over an hour late. I've been ringing your apartment on and off for the last thirty minutes. I thought something had happened to you. Or that you might have taken it into your head to resign again.'

'Re-resign?' she repeated blankly, one arm partially pulled out of the sleeve of her coat. 'Why should I want to resign?'

Dark brows lifted, he moved lithely to assist her with the outer garment. 'Given my recent behaviour, I'd say you might have several good reasons.'

'I . . .' Good Lord, was he offering some oblique form of apology for the unpredictable treatment he'd been meting out? It seemed a very uncharacteristic thing for him to do and yet, there was a rueful gentleness in his face that struck her as genuine. 'It's . . . all right,' she faltered. 'That is, I didn't—It is all right. Honestly.'

He draped her coat over the arm of a chair, brushing

the smooth fabric with his fingers. There was a strange
uneasiness about him. 'I was . . . concerned about you
this morning,' he said slowly, almost as though he found
the idea a disturbing one.

'I—I appreciate that,' she returned. 'And I'm sorry
you were worried. But, as you can see, I'm fine.'
She gave a comic little shrug, seeking some kind of
equilibrium.

Predictably, Michael found his bearings first, his uneasiness disappearing like smoke before a breeze.

'Your hair is coming down,' he observed prosaically.

'What? Oh—' She grimaced in irritation. She'd completely forgotten that, after her mad sprint from the
subway, she probably looked like a windswept mess. She
raised one hand to assess the damage.

'It's beyond repair,' Michael stated flatly, sweeping
her fingers aside. 'Turn round.'

'I'm perfectly capable—'

'I know that, Miss Whitney.' He placed pointedly
ironic stress on her name. 'I don't doubt that given ten or
fifteen minutes, you could screw your hair back into that
damn bun you insist on wearing. But we're running
behind schedule already this morning, so we don't have
time for that.'

Gritting her teeth, she turned her back to him. What
was she supposed to do? Compared with Michael's
changeable nature, a weathervane caught in a tornado
was a paragon of stability!

He plucked the remaining pins out of the wreckage of
her once-tidy chignon and pocketed them. With a sense
of resignation, Shauna felt her hair tumble loose and
free over her shoulders.

'Better,' Michael declared.

She turned back to face him, taking a step back as she
did so. Unbidden, she recalled what he had said that
night up in Hartford about how men—how he!—
responded to pinned up hair and buttoned up garments.
The rosy colour in her cheeks deepened at the memory.

'Do "we" have time for me to at least brush my

hair?' she enquired waspishly. 'I probably look like I just—'

'Woke up?' he supplied helpfully as she abruptly swallowed the remainder of her remark. He considered this just long enough to underscore the fact that he had some basis for judging how she looked when she'd just woken up. Then he went on with suave generosity, 'Brush your hair if you want to, Shauna, then bring your pad into my office. I've got some dictation about my meeting yesterday with Mr Kelso.'

'Some' dictation turned out to be a fluent ninety minutes of rapid-fire commentary punctuated by succinct directives to key people in all of SEE's major departments. Shauna was trembling but triumphant when Michael finally came to a halt. Despite a cramp in her hand, she'd kept up with his dizzying, dynamic pace. She felt a surge of renewed energy when he tossed her a flashing grin of approval.

She returned to her desk, her chestnut hair rippling softly about her shoulders, and set to work typing. No sooner had she deciphered the first paragraph of her shorthand than she was interrupted by a series of phone calls. Then came an invasion from the Sales Department, complete with graphs and charts.

Things slowed down in the late afternoon and she applied herself with a will, determined to finish the transcription before she left for the weekend. It was near her usual going home time when the telephone rang yet again.

'Mr Sebastian's office,' she said automatically, frowning over a squiggled notation on her pad.

'This is Lynette Cord.' The voice was flat and unfamiliar.

'Yes?' Now, what *did* that scrawl mean?

'I want to speak to Michael.'

Shauna glanced toward Michael's office. He'd been closeted in there, by himself, with the door shut, for the last hour.

'Ah—Mr Sebastian is in conference right now,' she

said politely. 'Perhaps there's something I can do? I'm his—'

'I'm his mother. I want to speak with him. It's important.'

Shauna's fingers tightened around the phone. 'One —one moment, please.' She pressed the 'hold' button before the woman on the other end of the line could speak.

Lynette Cord! Michael's *mother* . . . and Jamie's, too, of course. But why would she be calling?

With a sense of foreboding, Shauna rang through to Michael on the inter-office line.

'Yes?'

'Michael, there's a woman on line eight who says she's your mother—'

'My mother?' There was a razor sharpness to the question.

'Her name is Lynette Cord. She wants to speak with you. She says it's important . . .' She paused, hoping for some response. 'I—I told her you were in conference,' she went on. 'If you want—'

'No. No, Shauna, I'll take her call.' He disconnected abruptly. A second or so later, the hold signal on her phone console stopped flashing, indicating that he had picked up the phone.

The light for line eight blinked off less than five minutes later, signalling the end of the conversation. Unconsciously, Shauna tensed, half-expecting a summons from Michael. When none came, she forced her mind back to the task at hand.

She typed steadily for another hour, heaving a sigh when she finally completed her task. She'd just finished checking the last page when the inter-office line rang. Her heart gave a curious lurch as she picked up.

'Shauna?' Michael's voice was flat. 'Dee keeps a bottle of aspirin tucked away in one of her desk drawers. Would you please bring me a couple and some water?'

'Ah—Yes, of course.'

'Thanks.'

Two minutes later, she entered Michael's office with the aspirin and the water plus the papers she had typed.

Michael was sitting at his desk, his dark head slightly bent, his fingers steepled in front of his face and his thumbs pressed under his chin. He seemed lost in thought, his expression shuttered.

Quietly, Shauna crossed the thickly carpeted floor and placed the aspirin bottle and the glass of water on his desk. After a moment, he acknowledged her presence with a nod. He then opened the plastic container and shook out two aspirin. He popped the tablets down with a quick swallow of water.

'Would you like something else?' Shauna asked. Michael's office was decorated in the same starkly contemporary elegance of the reception area. It included a well-stocked smoked-glass and chrome bar. Her eyes strayed in that direction for an instant.

He gave a humourless laugh. His tie had been loosened sometime earlier. Pulling it off now with an impatient gesture, he tossed it carelessly aside. He undid the top two buttons of his white silk shirt.

'Do you think I need a drink, Miss Whitney?' he enquired, fixing her with hard jade eyes.

'No, of course not,' she replied quietly. He looked tired, she thought. Almost exhausted. She could see the signs of stress in the set of his lean features.

She was taken aback by the sudden rush of hostility she felt towards Lynette Cord.

Michael raked his fingers back through his hair. 'Did you stay late on my account?' he asked, a hint of challenge in his tone.

She lifted her chin. 'I—I stayed to finish the dictation you gave me,' she answered steadily, placing the papers she had typed on his desk in a neat stack. 'I thought you'd want to check them over the weekend.'

'Very commendable.' He flipped through several of the pages, his expression neutral. 'Very commendable.' He closed his eyes for a moment, tilting his head forward with a small grunt. He massaged one shoulder and then the other. 'There are a few things a man can't do for himself,' he observed in a wry undertone.

'Perhaps I could help—' Shauna began impulsively. She broke off as his head came up.

'Yes?' One dark brow quirked questioningly as he prompted her.

'I could try to loosen the muscles for you,' she finished, knowing she was colouring under his scrutiny. She strove for a light note. 'I don't have much experience as a masseuse, but typing is supposed to give a person strong hands.'

For a moment, she thought he was going to laugh at her—or reject her suggestion with a cutting retort. Her blush deepened painfully.

'That's the best offer I've had in a long time,' he said slowly. 'I'd appreciate your . . . ministrations.'

She could feel the tension in him when she placed her fingers lightly on his shoulders and began to massage the taut muscles she found there. While the fine silk of his shirt had a sleek, expensive quality to it, she was more aware of the heated texture of the skin beneath.

In the first minute or so, there was absolutely no give in him. If anything, he seemed to stiffen against the pressure of her hands as though resisting her touch. Then, as though she'd found a hidden nerve, he expelled a long breath and began to relax a little.

With increased confidence, Shauna started to knead the tendons on either side of his neck. The stroking rhythms of her slender fingers were slow but steady.

Shauna's parents had been warmly demonstrative people. Her early childhood had been full of affectionate cuddling. Her adolescence had been coldly different. Her Aunt Margaret had rejected physical contact with undisguised distaste. Because of this, Shauna had learned to school and finally suppress her natural urges . . . to deny her own blossoming sensuality.

Now, she discovered herself revelling in the feel of Michael's unmistakably male flesh. The broad shoulders and strongly sculpted neck pleased her hands. She was conscious of a sense of intimate satisfaction as she felt some of the strain ease out of him.

'Aren't you curious?' he asked, finally breaking the silence between them. His voice was low.

'Curious?' she repeated absently, moving her thumbs up the back of his neck, brushing at the thick dark hair that grew at his nape.

'Hmm . . . yes. The call from Lynette Cord. My mother.' There was acid contempt in the overly precise way he pronounced the last two words.

'It really isn't any of my business,' Shauna replied quietly, her hands going still. 'I just hope it wasn't bad news.'

'That depends on your point of view. She called to tell me she's getting married again.'

'I . . . Oh.'

'I suppose I should be grateful she's past the age of child-bearing,' he added gratingly. He swivelled his chair, looking up at her. 'Does that shock you?'

She pressed her palms against her skirt. 'No,' she admitted with candid simplicity.

He regarded her narrowly for several seconds.

'Jamie must have had a great deal to say to you that Saturday morning up in Hartford,' he observed flatly.

Shauna shifted awkwardly, worrying her bottom lip with her teeth. 'He told me she—your mother—wasn't very maternal.'

'True.' His lips twisted scornfully.

'Before that . . . when he asked me to spend the weekend with Tempest . . . he told me that she'd deserted you. That is, it slipped out in response to something I said. But I wasn't prying—'

'I know that. You don't need to pry.' He exhaled wearily. 'My mother. She used her pregnancy with me to get my father to marry her. She used him as her ticket out of the small town existence she hated. I was nine when she finally walked out for good. Old enough to know what was going on, but too damn young to do anything about it.' He shook his head as though fighting off the memory. 'My father genuinely loved her. Even after he got the papers saying she'd divorced him, he still harboured this fantasy that one day she'd come back, and we'd be a happy family again. Of course, we were never much of a family in the first place.'

Shauna's heart constricted. 'But, in the end, after your father died—?'

'Are you asking if she had a change of heart towards me? No. Jamie's father was the one who made the decision to take me in instead of dumping me into some foster home. He was . . . a decent man. Although his decency was wasted on me, I'm afraid.'

'I don't believe that,' she protested.

His brows went up. 'No? Well, after seven years of knocking around the country on the fringes of the music business, I didn't quite fit into his nice, middle-class view of life. Oh, he meant well enough. I suppose he wanted to give me the chance to be an ordinary sixteen-year-old kid. What he couldn't—or wouldn't—understand was that, at sixteen, I'd already seen more of life than most men twice that age. I lost my innocence young. Probably the day I realised that the world is made up of people who get used and those who use them . . . and decided I wasn't going to be one of the former if there was anything I could do to prevent it.'

Innocence. Something in his voice as he said the word betrayed a profound regret. He was not ashamed of his past, yet Shauna sensed that he was bitterly aware of how much it had cost him.

'Of course, you pay a price for that kind of decision,' he went on levelly, seeming to discern her line of thinking. 'The real reason my mother called was to make sure her monthly allowance cheque would be made out in her new name from now on.'

'You—you give her an allowance?' Shauna didn't think she'd heard correctly. 'You help support her?'

'I pay her,' he amended. 'Don't interpret it as some noble act of generosity. Seven years ago, money was the lever I used to get her to agree that Jamie should be released into my custody. Since then—' he shrugged negligently. 'One of the things she used to throw at me when she got angry during that year I lived with the Cords was that I was just like my father. I'd never amount to anything, either, she'd say. Whether she knows it or not, I'm throwing those words back at her with each monthly cheque she takes from me.'

'Do you ever see her?'

He shook his head. 'No. It's a little late for that, don't you think?'

'I . . . suppose . . .' An odd combination of feelings was welling up inside her. Compassion for the boy he must have been . . . understanding for the man he had become . . . and something deeper and far more abiding.

'You Made Me What I Am'. The title of Michael's first hit flashed through her mind. Yet, for all the anger in that song, it was more a clear-eyed appraisal of reality than a finger-pointing catalogue of blame.

He was tough, cynical, and ambitious. But there was so much more to him than that: so much his forced maturity might have destroyed or warped.

There was the artistic sensitivity she'd discovered that morning in his apartment when he'd woven his music with her words. There was the personal strength and the professional integrity she'd come to recognise during the past week.

So much to know, to admire. So much to—love?

'Shauna, will you have dinner with me?'

She stared at him, more shaken by her realisation of the inevitable conclusion of her train of thought than by his totally unexpected invitation. 'Dinner?' she got out. 'But why?'

His smile was wry. 'Because it's late. Because I'm hungry. And because it's what I want.'

And what you want, you get. She didn't say it; not because she didn't believe it, but because she heard the self-mockery in his final sentence.

'Please,' he added quietly, rising from his chair. For a

moment, he seemed on the verge of reaching out to her to underline his invitation, but something held him back. He stood, his gaze sharply watchful, allowing her to make up her own mind.

She wanted to go with him. That, for the moment at least, was all that mattered to her.

'I'm hungry, too,' she declared.

He took her to the Russian Tea Room near Carnegie Hall. Shauna had walked by the restaurant many times, fascinated by its garishly dramatic window displays and by the glamorous people she saw sweeping in and out through the gilt-decorated revolving front door.

'Have you ever been here before?' Michael asked conversationally as they were seated.

Shauna shook her head, looking around with interest. She spotted several celebrities, including a famous ballet dancer who had defected from the Soviet Union. She was conscious that Michael was drawing interested glances from a number of the patrons; after all, he was a celebrity in his own right, too.

'It's an amazing place,' she commented with un-affected appreciation. 'It's like being inside a Christmas ornament.' In the front of the restaurant, scarlet banquettes contrasted gaily with pink table linen. Further back, deep green walls sprouted a collection of apparently haphazardly hung oil paintings and brightly polished samovars. The chandeliers and sconces which lighted the room were cheerfully draped with strands of gold and silver tinsel.

Michael smiled. 'There's no place like it,' he agreed, accepting a menu from a waiter clad in a red cossack-style shirt. 'Do you want something to drink?'

'White wine, please.'

He ordered vodka for himself, making a quip about adhering to Russian tradition. He also asked for a plate of *pirozhki*. Shauna found the piping hot pastries—stuffed with spicy chopped meat and onions—absolutely delicious.

Although the translations on the back of the menu made each dish sound like something fit for a Tsar, Shauna decided on the classic chicken Kiev. Michael ordered blini with red caviar and sour cream. Both dishes were presented at their table with a little flourish. After placing Shauna's plate in front of her, their waiter deftly thrust a small knife into the centre of her chicken, releasing a golden spurt of melted herbed butter on to the accompanying bed of fluffy white rice.

'It's wonderful,' she said after sampling it.

'I thought you'd like this place,' Michael observed, tasting his own selection.

She glanced at him questioningly. 'You picked this restaurant because of me?'

'It's not one of my regular haunts,' he conceded. 'But I hoped the atmosphere would appeal to you.'

'Oh.' She took a sip of white wine, a faint line of puzzlement appearing between her brows.

'Here, see if this appeals,' Michael offered lightly, extending a mouthful of his entrée across the table on the prongs of his fork. Feeling a bit conspicuous, Shauna leaned forward and accepted the morsel, savouring the delicate flavour of the buckwheat pancake, the tang of the sour cream, and the unfamiliar saltiness of the caviar.

'Very good,' she told him, sitting back. She brushed a strand of hair back over her shoulder, still wondering about his previous comment. Having checked through Michael's appointment calendar on numerous occasions during the past week, she knew he patronised many of New York City's most outstanding restaurants—although she suspected that making deals, not merely dining out, was the reason for his endless round of lunches and dinners. She had assumed he'd chosen the Russian Tea Room because it was fairly near SEE and because he personally favoured it. That, it seemed, was not so.

'I wrote a song about food once,' he volunteered with a crooked smile. It was the first personal comment he'd made since they'd left the office. 'I was about eleven or so at the time. It was in praise of ice cream and hamburgers.'

'Not filet mignon and champagne?' she joked casually.

'No. I had very simple tastes as a kid. That was all I could afford.' For a moment, she heard echoes of the revelations he had made to her earlier. She wondered if he regretted telling her so much about himself.

'You—you draw on your own life a lot when you write your music, don't you? she asked with a mixture of curiosity and hesitation.

He swallowed the last bite of his food and set down his fork with a precise gesture. 'No more than you do when you write your poetry,' he countered, then frowned as she stiffened. 'No, damn it, don't do that!' he snapped with unexpected intensity. His green eyes darkened to jade.

'Don't do what?'

'Don't pull back. One moment you're all warmth and openness, then wham, Miss Whitney's back with a vengeance. You're always holding something back.'

Shauna toyed with her fork, pushing a few remaining grains of rice around on her place. 'A girl doesn't want to give away all her secrets,' she responded after a moment, managing to keep her voice light.

'There's a difference between keeping secrets and building walls, Shauna.'

She looked at him. 'What about you?' she parried.

'What—'

'Don't you build walls? Don't you draw a line around yourself saying "so far and no farther"?' She was thinking of the moments when he'd suddenly, without explanation, broken the line of communication that had sprung up between them. How many times had he breached her defences and drawn her towards him only to throw up his own barriers at the last moment, shutting her out?

His jaw tightened. There was anger, frustration, and

something else in his expression. 'I have my reasons,' he said after a strained silence.

Her hazel eyes were lambent with vulnerability. 'Maybe I do, too,' she answered, with a catch in her voice.

They were interrupted then by their waiter, who began clearing the table with the efficiency of long experience. His task accomplished, he asked Michael if there was anything else they wanted.

'Would you like any dessert?' Michael looked at Shauna, his manner smooth and controlled.

She clenched her hands under the table. Challenging him had taken an unnerving amount of boldness; she wasn't ready to pursue the matter . . . not now.

'No, thank you,' she replied politely, following Michael's lead. 'But—I would like some tea, please.'

'Tea for the lady and a brandy for me,' he instructed the waiter.

There was a small pause. It lengthened to the point of becoming awkward—even tense—before the waiter returned.

'Thank you,' Shauna murmured. The tea was served in a glass set in a handled, wrought-metal holder. She took a few moments to slowly stir in a packet of sugar before looking across the table at Michael. He was making a small circular pattern on the tablecloth with his brandy goblet.

'I have a confession to make,' he said, his mouth twisting. He tasted the amber liqueur in his glass. 'I had an ulterior motive for inviting you to dinner tonight.'

'Ulterior motive?' She didn't even attempt to keep the wariness out of her voice.

'Don't worry. I'm not plotting your seduction . . . at least not tonight.' As her heart performed an alarming flip-flop in response to this remark, he reached inside the breast pocket of his suit jacket and withdrew several folded sheets of paper.

'What—?'

'Lead sheets,' he told her, unfolding the papers. He

smoothed them out on the table, face up. 'I wrote them out myself. When I was starting out, I used to do this sort of thing to supplement what I was earning washing dishes. It was as good a way as any to get contacts . . . I'm lucky enough to have a good natural ear for melodies and legible handwriting.'

Shauna bit her lip painfully as she realised what the sheets were. Boldly inked-in notes danced across musical staves . . . words, lettered in an angular masculine hand, marched evenly beneath the notes.

'My poem.'

'My music. Our song.'

Our song. The quietly spoken assertion sent a powerful shaft of emotion through her. Her eyes settled on the top of the first sheet of paper. Although it bore no title, it did carry their names, paired together in strong script, in the right-hand corner.

Michael reached across the table, his musician's fingers closing over one of her hands. 'I've been carrying these around since—well, for nearly two weeks. I've been wanting to share them with you.'

'And then what?' The touch of his fingers was sure, gentle, and strong.

He leaned forward. 'I know what your poetry means to you. I also know it can mean something to other people. Shauna, the music I used for this—the tune I played for you—it's something I wrote a long time ago. It means something to me. I always knew it was supposed to be a song, but I could never come up with the right words for it. And I tried. Believe me, I tried.' He smiled briefly. 'Some of the best lyrics I've ever written didn't work with this music. Then I read your poem and I knew . . . I *knew*.'

'You want me to agree to let you use my—lyrics.'

'Yes,' he said simply. 'We've made a good song together. It would be a shame not to have it sung so other people can hear it.'

She took a sip of her tea. 'Do—do you have to have an answer right now?' She'd given him her answer once before, and it had been no. She'd been so certain it would always be no.

Michael shook his head, releasing her hand. 'I can wait. I'm learning to be a patient man about some things.' He took a swallow of his brandy. 'Keep the lead sheets. No matter what you finally decide, they're yours. I've got my own copy.'

About fifteen minutes later, he escorted her out into the night. They walked silently to Sixth Avenue where he flagged down a passing cab.

'I hope you don't mind if we share,' he said, sliding into the black vinyl back seat next to her and pulling the door shut. 'The driver can let you out first.'

'That's fine, thank you. I live at—'

'I know, remember?' he cut in smoothly. Leaning forward, he told the driver her address.

The ride was a stop-start journey up the West Side. As they neared her apartment building, Shauna felt a rising sense of anxiety. Would they go through a repeat of their Wednesday night parting? What did he expect from her at this point?

They were long past a simple employer-employee relationship . . . if they could be said to have ever had one in the first place. Surely that confrontation in the studio—and what had followed from it—had put them on something other than a professional footing!

As for their personal footing . . . they weren't really friends, and they certainly weren't lovers. But there was an intimate bonding, none the less.

Finally, Shauna shifted to look at Michael. 'Well,' she said, clearing her throat. 'Thank you for a—a lovely evening. I enjoyed the Russian Tea Room very much. I'm glad you thought of it.'

Michael studied her for a moment, a gentle gleam of amusement in his eyes as he read the uncertainty that shadowed her face. The jade green of his gaze softened slightly.

'Thank you,' he returned quietly. There was a moment's hesitation on his part. Then, with infinite care, he reached for her. Gathering her close, he bent his dark head and kissed her.

The taste and touch of him had a heady familiarity. As his mouth closed over hers—gently at first, then with deepening hunger—Shauna realised she had relived his previous kisses many times. She now knew the velvet soft caress of his lips and the teasing probe of his tongue . . . knew the way they helped define the shape and sweetness of her own yielding mouth.

'Michael—' she breathed, giving herself up to the sensations he was arousing. Even through the cloth of her coat, she could feel the warmth coming off his body. It sparked an answering heat within her. The passions she had conjured up and poured into her writing were throbbing inside her, clamouring with aching eagerness for a new release.

'Hey, mister, you gonna get out or do you want I should take it around the block a few times?'

This nonchalant question came from the cabbie. Shaken, Shauna pulled away from Michael, her cheeks scarlet. The taxi had come to a full stop in front of her building. Knowing her face would betray the physical tumult within her, she did not dare look at Michael.

Trembling, she glanced at the driver, who'd half turned round when he'd made his casually jocular enquiry. The man gave her an understanding wink as if to assure her he was beyond being shocked by anything that went on in the back seat of a New York City cab.

'Actually,' Michael said in a calm voice, dropping a quick, butterfly light kiss on the corner of her mouth before completely relinquishing his hold on her. 'Actually, the lady is getting out here. I'm going on.' He reached across Shauna and opened the door for her, his lean torso pressing briefly against the upper part of her body.

Still quivering, she climbed out of the cab, astonished to find that her legs could still support her.

'Good night, Shauna,' he said.

'Good night,' she echoed, her hand on the door

handle. She felt dazed. Impulse prompted her to bend down and look back inside the taxi. 'Michael . . . how old were you when you wrote the music to that—our song?' The question came out in a rush, seemingly of its own volition.

He did not reply immediately. 'I was seventeen and a half,' he replied at last. He did not ask why she wanted to know.

'I . . . see. Good night again, Michael.' She shut the door and stepped back. A moment later, the driver eased the car into the rushing flow of night traffic. Shauna stood watching from the pavement, the chill autumn wind plucking at her hair, until the cab turned the corner and sped out of sight.

She had to force herself to breathe. She was acutely aware of the beating of her heart and the insistent pounding of her pulse.

The Shauna Whitney her Aunt Margaret had tried to mould—the one she had dutifully tried to be for half her life—knew it wasn't possible to fall in love with a man she had really only known for a week.

The Shauna Whitney she *was* knew that was precisely what she'd done.

CHAPTER EIGHT

KNOWING—and admitting it to herself—made everything harder.

It had been much easier before, when she had been able to tell herself that what she felt for Michael Sebastian was either something as impersonal as admiration . . . or as transitory as physical attraction. She did admire him as a musician, and she was attracted to him as a man . . . but there was more than that. Much, much more.

She loved him.

For Shauna, love meant commitment—marriage and a family. Despite the cold shadow her aunt had cast over her life, she'd clung to the loving example her parents had set when she was a little girl. She'd always hoped that she could have with a man what they had shared as husband and wife.

Instead, she'd given her heart to a man from a broken home who freely admitted he'd learned, with good reason, to distrust women from a very early age. A man whose music sang of momentary passions and seduced with no promises of tomorrow.

And a man who was involved with another woman. Despite the fragment of telephone conversation she had overheard on Friday, Shauna had no illusions about the relationship between Michael Sebastian and Carla Decker. Carla no doubt gave him exactly what he wanted from a woman.

What would this man do if he knew he had her heart? That was something Shauna did not intend to find out. Michael already had too many weapons to turn against her if he chose. He had learned too many of her vulnerabilities.

The poem she had written had a bitter-sweet irony to

it now. Her heart was no longer untouched; it was no longer hers to keep. She had given it, unasked and in secret. Yet she was still alone, apart . . . an island.

Refusing to let Michael use that poem seemed more imperative than ever before. The blending of her words and his music was just too intimate to be made public. And if she said yes to him once . . . could she ever say no again?

With Aunt Margaret's stern dictates about idle hands and dangerous thoughts echoing in her head, Shauna did her best to keep busy over the weekend. But the endless round of minor household tasks and errands she found to do was an ineffective distraction at best.

She dressed for work with particular care on Monday. Her first impulse had been to retreat to the safe, restrained style to which she had clung for so long, but she discovered she could not. Michael's repeated jibes about 'Miss Whitney' had hit home and struck deep. He'd made her see how she used her appearance as a defence against life and as a denial of what she felt inside. If 'Miss Whitney' returned, he'd know it was because Shauna had something to hide and she suspected he'd probe until he found out what it was.

But that wasn't the only reason she took such pains with her looks. She discovered, as she stood staring at her reflection in the bathroom mirror, that she couldn't bring herself to step back into the narrow and confining boundaries her aunt had tried to teach her were 'proper'. She also discovered that she wanted to look attractive for Michael. She wanted to provoke that emerald flare of interest in his eyes . . . that slow, teasing smile of appreciation he sometimes gave her.

She got just the reaction she was hoping for when she brought him his morning coffee and a stack of neatly sorted mail.

'New dress, Shauna?' he asked, leaning back in his chair, his long, jeans-clad legs stretched out in front of him as he surveyed her with half-lidded eyes. He wore a white linen shirt, a Harris tweed jacket, and running shoes. A black leather belt with a heavy, handcrafted brass buckle circled his narrow waist, emphasising his masculine fitness. Even if she hadn't already consulted his crowded appointment schedule, his casual appearance would have tipped her off that the day was going to be devoted to artistic matters, not strictly business concerns.

She shook her head, covertly searching his face for any sign that his weekend had been a troubled one, too. She could find none.

'No,' she said. 'You just haven't seen it before.' The dress she was wearing was a soft, rust wool jersey, simply styled and infinitely flattering to the soft curves of her body. Instead of using the narrow matching belt, she'd wrapped her waist with a bronze, brown, and cream striped silk scarf. She'd swept her hair up into a loose topknot, leaving tendrils free at the nape of her neck and at her temples. Gold knot earrings and several slender gold chains at her throat completed the outfit.

'Well, I'd like to see more of it,' he told her. 'If you're attempting to make me forget my rule about Mondays, you're on the right track.'

'Your rule about Mondays?' she repeated, puzzled.

'The one about not seducing employees. Remember? I mentioned it the day you came to my apartment.'

Her lashes fell for a moment as she made an effort to hide her sudden surge of emotion. 'How—how could I forget?' she returned wryly after a few seconds, unthinkingly twisting the free ends of the scarf she had knotted around her waist.

'I certainly haven't,' he commented with a brief but devastatingly sexy smile. 'Did you want something else?' he enquired. 'Other than to have me admire your dress, I mean.'

She took a deep breath, mentally squaring her shoulders. 'I . . . wanted to talk about Friday.'

He picked up his coffee and took a sip. His eyes were very intent. 'Do you want me to apologise?'

Her eyes widened with bewilderment. 'For what?'

'Kissing you.'

'Why should you do that?' she responded. 'It wasn't the first time you kissed me. You never apologised before.'

There was a short but pregnant pause. Shauna swallowed, wishing she could take back the ill-advised words. His suggestion had been so far from what she had expected that she'd simply blurted out the first thing that came into her head.

'You're right,' he agreed quietly. 'Do I take it you'd like me to go back to the beginning of our—ah—relationship and start apologising from there?'

She met his gaze evenly for a few seconds then dropped her eyes, unnerved by the intensity of his expression. He knows, she thought. Somehow, he knows!

'You don't have to apologise,' she said finally. 'Nothing happened. No harm done.'

'Are you certain?'

'Yes!' What was he driving at?

'I see.'

She twisted her hands together. 'Michael—what I want to talk about is the . . . our . . . song.'

He expelled his breath very slowly. 'You want to tell me the answer's still no, is that it?'

She nodded.

'Sit down, Shauna,' he instructed softly.

'I don't—' She wanted to get out of the office.

'Please.'

She complied hesitantly, taking one of the chairs across the desk from him.

'You know the song's good, don't you?' he asked persuasively. 'That we're good together?'

His choice of words sent a peculiar tremor through her. It also strengthened her resolve. 'I just can't,' she told him.

'Or you just won't.'

'Either way, the answer's still no.' She had the feeling they were talking a code she couldn't decipher. If

Michael possessed the key, he wasn't about to share it. 'Please, try to understand.'

'I understand better than you think,' he shot back, running a hand through his hair. 'Shauna, are you ashamed of what you wrote? Are you ashamed of what you felt when you wrote—'

'No!' Appalled, she started to get to her feet. Michael rose out of his chair in the same instant, reaching out across the desk in a gesture of appeal.

'Don't,' he said harshly.

The urgency in his voice stopped her. She froze like a wild, frightened creature on the verge of flight.

'Don't,' he repeated in a more moderate tone. 'I'm sorry. I don't know what I said—I'm sorry.'

'I'm not ashamed of my poetry,' she declared in a low, steady voice. 'But I told you before, it's *private*. That's just the way I feel. I can't help it.'

He gave a brief, bitter laugh. 'No, I don't suppose you can. Any more than I can help—' He stopped.

'Any more than you can help . . . what?'

'Shauna, my whole life has been a matter of seeing what I wanted, going after it, and getting it. I never learned how to wait for something to be given instead of taking it.'

'But you've said you always get what you want.'

'Not quite always.'

Confused hazel eyes met direct, darkening green ones. The message Shauna read in Michael's face made her breath stop at the top of her throat. Inexperienced as she was, she recognised that they were no longer talking about her poetry.

Michael wanted *her*.

She soared on a brief, explosive moment of happiness before reality sent her crashing back to earth.

He *wanted* her . . . just as he had probably wanted dozens of other women. Yes, he felt something for her, but it was the kind of feeling he had described in the song he had written for Tempest. It was the kind of feeling that drew two people together for a night and then burned itself into meaningless oblivion with the coming of the morning.

Better he should feel nothing at all for her.

And was she even the one he really wanted? It had been her poetry that attracted him. He wanted the woman who'd written the poem—he wanted a Shauna Whitney in the image of his own choosing, just as her Aunt Margaret had.

'The answer is no, Michael.'

The hot, disturbingly hungry look vanished from his eyes as completely as if it had never been there in the first place. It was as though he'd thrown a switch inside himself.

'All right,' he replied. 'To every rule there is an exception. You, Miss Whitney, seem destined to be mine.'

'I'm sorry.' She spoke almost defensively, and that made her angry.

He shook his head. 'You don't have to apologise,' he said, echoing the words she had said to him only minutes before. 'No harm done.'

'Do you understand . . . about the song?'

'All too well.'

'I'll—I'll give you back the lead sheets if you want them,' she offered awkwardly.

'No. I told you those were yours, no matter what you finally decided.' His mouth twisted mockingly. 'I admit I hoped they might turn the trick. Seeing something written down, tangible, sometimes makes a difference. It can convince you something's real. But—' He spread his hands and shrugged. 'In any case, as I also told you, I've got my own copy. Right here.' He pulled open his top desk drawer, gesturing. His expression changed slightly and he reached in. He took something out of the drawer and extended the object to Shauna on his open palm.

For a moment she just stared. Then she gave a surprised ripple of laughter.

'My glasses!' she exclaimed, genuinely taken aback. She felt as though she were looking at a souvenir from some previous existence. 'I'd—I'd almost forgotten about them,' she admitted honestly as she took them from his hand.

'I hope you won't go back to wearing them.'

'I won't.' It came out firm and certain.

'Good. I've got something else of yours, too.'

It was the manila envelope containing her poetry. He placed it on the desk top between them. Shauna looked down at it silently, a small part of her mind registering the fingermarks and smudges on the outer edges of the packet. It looked as though it had been handled and opened repeatedly. She glanced at him questioningly, an alarming thought occurring to her. What if he had—?

'Don't worry,' he said, seeming to reach to the core of her thoughts. 'No one else has read them but me. Your secrets are safe. They're all here.'

'Thank you.' She picked up the envelope.

'Well, then, I think that's it.' He drummed his fingers lightly against the top of the desk. 'Shall we get to work?'

'Yes. Yes, of course.' She wondered why she didn't feel more elated at getting her poems back. Turning, she walked towards the door.

'Shauna.'

She looked back at him. 'Yes?'

'Don't throw that envelope—or what's in it—at anybody else,' he told her softly. 'Please.'

'I—I won't,' she promised him solemnly, and hurried out of the office. 'I won't,' she repeated under her breath.

The rest of the day was hectic, giving her little time to brood about what had transpired between them. In many ways, she was grateful for this; she did not want to dwell on the disturbing implications of what she had seen in his eyes.

The pace slowed a bit in the late afternoon. She used the break to dash down to the employees' cafeteria and pick up a piece of fruit from one of the vending machines. She'd had no time for lunch.

Crunching on a mouthful of crisp apple, she raced back to her desk. The buzzer on the inter-office line sounded as she sank back into her seat.

'Yes?'

'Where were you?'

'Getting something to eat,' she replied. 'I missed lunch.'

'You also missed a telephone call.'

'What?'

'Come in and I'll tell you.'

Puzzled, Shauna did as instructed. Michael was standing with his back to the door, his dark head tilted consideringly as he studied the row of dummy album covers he had lined up on the window ledge behind his desk. The mock-ups ranged from an abstract starburst of vivid colour to a dramatic close-up of Jamie Cord's face. Each bore the name Tempest in lettering that matched the logo on the T-shirt she'd been given in Hartford.

But it was Michael himself that held her attention. He'd discarded his tweed jacket and, as he crossed his arms in front of him, the fabric of his shirt tautened, hinting at the play of muscles on his shoulders and back. The snug fit of his jeans was even more revealing as he shifted his weight restlessly.

As if sensing her presence he turned, casually hooking his thumbs into his belt. 'What do you think?' he asked.

She walked over to him, acutely conscious of the movement of her body in relation to his. 'About the albums?'

He nodded. 'Tempest has a gig on Long Island over the weekend and then they're doing some studio work on the new album on Monday. I wanted to show them what we've got in mind for the cover.'

'I can guess which one Jamie will like best,' she commented with a laugh.

He grinned. 'So can I.'

'What will Griz, Sam, Hank and Frank think of it?'

'If we use the one with the close-up of Jamie, their

pictures will go on the back of the cover. It's not exactly equal billing, but they're smart enough to understand the realities of the situation.'

'I suppose so. Is this picture by the same photographer who has the new rock-and-roll history book coming out?'

'*On the Road and Never Coming Back?* Yes. You've got a good eye.'

'I—I liked the portrait he took of you.'

'You've seen it?' He seemed surprised.

'It was in a magazine,' she explained. The black and white study had been unposed and emphatically informal, capturing Michael backstage at a concert. The show business chaos surrounding him had seemed oddly insubstantial in comparison with the controlled energy and utter assurance he projected. 'It reminds me of the way you looked that night I came to deliver the contracts for Mr Barkley.'

'That bad?' His tone was mocking. 'I had the distinct impression my looks turned you off that night, Miss Whitney.'

'There was nothing wrong with the way you looked,' she retorted, stung. 'It was what you did.'

To her surprise, he laughed. 'And you said I didn't have anything to apologise for.'

Shauna took a deep breath, knowing she was being deliberately baited and recognising how dangerous it was to be drawn into whatever game he was playing. 'You said something about a phone call, Mr Sebastian?'

His green eyes glinted gold. 'Jamie called you.'

'He did?' She smiled with undisguised delight.

His features hardened as he took in her response. 'That's right. I'm supposed to tell you that Tempest misses your inspiration and is ready to have you rejoin them on the road. All expenses paid, of course.'

'Paid by whom?' She gave a little laugh.

'By SEE, I'd imagine. Isn't that what happened the last time?' Although his tone was bland, there were devils dancing in the depths of his eyes as though he was remembering, in vivid detail, all of what had happened 'the last time'.

'It's your company,' she returned. 'What did you say to the idea?'

'I told him you'd consider it,' he replied coolly. 'Jamie also said he hoped to be able to see you sometime during the weekend. And, naturally, you've got an open invitation to their performances.'

'I'd like that.'

He moved away from her abruptly, going to the window and beginning to collect the album covers. 'Had you heard from Jamie before this?' he asked, stacking the cardboard rectangles. There was something more than simple curiosity in his voice.

Silvery sparkles of amusement lightened Shauna's hazel eyes. 'Yes, as a matter of fact, I have.' She did not add that Jamie's previous effort at communication had consisted of a joke postcard that had apparently been written and signed collectively by all five members of Tempest. The message had been succinct: 'This is an ugly postcard for a beautiful lady. Wish you were here —wherever that is!'

Michael dropped the albums on his desk. 'I see,' he commented tersely.

'Is there anything else?' she enquired.

He frowned for a moment, appearing to be on the verge of saying something. 'Shauna, I—No.' He sat down at his desk. 'No, that's it.'

'Then I'll get back to my work. Thank you for passing along the message from Jamie.'

His brows came together. 'You're welcome.'

She was nearly out the door when his voice halted her. 'Shauna!'

'Yes?' She was a trifle wary now, uncertain of his mood and of what might have provoked it.

'There is one thing. Carla Decker is finishing an engagement at Lake Tahoe. Dee has a listing for a florist in her Rolodex. Call them and arrange for some flowers to be sent in my name. The usual order, the usual message. Have it put on my account.'

'The usual order,' she repeated. The light-heartedness she had known just a few minutes before dissolved.

'That's right. Two dozen red roses.'

Shauna's stomach knotted. What did you expect? her mind hissed. Did you think he'd send her a little bouquet from a street vendor like the one you found on your desk the first day? She bit her lip at the memory of those modest flowers. Through judicious pruning and careful rearrangement, she'd made at least a few of the blossoms last the entire working week.

She felt like a fool recalling that . . . a *jealous* fool!

Michael Sebastian and Carla Decker are lovers, she reminded herself. You're nothing to him, except a temporary secretary and an even more temporary diversion.

She tilted her chin slightly. 'I'll take care of it,' she said, and turned gracefully on her heel.

Tuesday passed fairly uneventfully. But on Wednesday, fresh from her successful engagement in Lake Tahoe, Carla Decker made an unexpected appearance. A discreet call from the lobby security guard gave Shauna a much appreciated warning about the singer's impending arrival and she braced herself for almost anything.

Carla swept in looking every inch the sexy star she was. From the tips of her artfully permed hair to the lizard-skin toes of her high-heeled boots, she radiated a knowing, dynamic appeal. She was dressed in black velvet designer jeans and a white silk blouse with a mink coat draped casually over her shoulders like a cape.

'Well, well, we meet again,' she greeted Shauna throatily, her pansy-hued eyes wide but assessing. 'I thought you were just temporary.'

Shauna rose from behind her desk, smoothing the skirt of her tweed suit as she did so. 'I am just temporary, as you put it, Miss Decker,' she said with quiet poise. 'Dee is coming back Monday.'

'Oh.'

'I'm afraid Mi—Mr Sebastian isn't here right now.'

'Really? And where is Michael?' Carla placed delicate emphasis on Michael's given name as though underlining her right to use it.

Shauna recalled Dee's VIP list: *Carla Decker— Immediate Access—any time, any place.*

'He's meeting with the production people from one of the cable television companies—'

'About the in-concert series?' Carla cut in smoothly. 'Of course, I should have remembered.' She paused, glancing about the work area with an obviously simulated air of curiosity. 'So, have you enjoyed your little stint with Michael?'

'The work has been very interesting.'

'You don't mind the long hours, I take it.'

'Long hours?'

'Late dinners at the Russian Tea Room, that sort of thing.'

Shauna stiffened. 'Mr Sebastian had something to discuss with me,' she answered.

'I can imagine. It's odd he picked such a public place, don't you think?' It's not one of his usual spots, you know. And it was the kind of place you were just bound to be seen together.'

'Miss Decker, I really don't know what you're talking about,' Shauna said evenly and reseated herself. She was tempted to simply turn away from the woman and begin typing, but she didn't quite have the nerve.

'I simply thought you should know that Michael and I had a little spat over the phone last week and his taking you to dinner was—well, you know.' She smiled with patent insincerity. 'Darling, at least a half dozen of my so-called friends called me up to tell me about your dinner, which was exactly what Michael knew would happen. And, of course, we made up our tiff—he even sent me flowers. Now, I don't blame *you* for a second. Michael can be absolutely devastating when he wants to . . . and he is so expert at tugging the heartstrings with those funny-sad stories about his childhood.'

Shauna's stomach knotted. The phone conversation
. . . the flowers . . . it all fitted so flawlessly. And so for
the other, as for the naïve feeling that Michael had
singled her out for his confidences—why had she been so
wilfully blind? Any man as experienced as Michael
Sebastian was bound to know how women responded to
the image of the vulnerable boy he had once been. It was
just another means of getting what he wanted. In her
case, given her own cold childhood, it had been an all too
obvious method of manipulation.

She swallowed. 'We discussed business.'

Carla gestured airily. 'Of course. I'm sure that's all it
was. I just didn't think it was fair to let you think—But,
perhaps you didn't. You seem very sensible. And it's not
as though you haven't seen how Michael is . . . how the
two of us are.'

The embrace in the lift and the morning-after kiss in
his apartment. Oh, yes, Shauna had seen how Michael
was. How he and Carla were.

'I appreciate your concern, Miss Decker, but it really
isn't necessary,' she said steadily. She had the impression the singer was a trifle disconcerted by her
poised reactions. 'Now, is there something I can do for
you? Would you like to leave a message?'

Carla clicked her tongue and glanced at her watch as
though debating with herself. 'Actually, I think I'll wait
for Michael. We've got some things to discuss about this
talk-show appearance I'm doing Friday night.'

'I'm not at all certain when he'll be back.'

The singer waved her beautifully manicured hands
dismissively. 'I'll make myself at home in his office.
There's no need to show me around. I know where
Michael keeps everything. I'm sure I'll find something to
occupy me.' She glided across the room, pausing long
enough to look at Shauna over her shoulder. 'I'll shut the
door so you won't have to worry about disturbing me
while you type or whatever,' she said and vanished into
Michael's office.

Shauna operated like a badly programmed automaton

during the next hour and a half. A stack of filing which normally would have required only ten minutes seemed to take forever as she discovered that her grasp of the basics of alphabetising had suddenly grown very shaky. She finally gave up on that and sat down to type up some correspondence.

'Such language, Miss Whitney. I'm shocked.'

She froze, caught in the act of yanking a ruined piece of stationery out of her typewriter as she gave vent to a singularly unladylike exclamation. Hot colour flooded up into her cheeks as she turned to face Michael.

He leaned forward, palms flat on the desk, watching her agitation with a mixture of amused sympathy and almost clinical interest. A lock of his thick, dark hair had curved down over his forehead. Shauna caught a hint of his distinctive masculine scent.

'I'm sorry,' she said abruptly, dropping her eyes. She crumpled the paper up into a ball and tossed it into the waste-basket.

He no longer looked amused. 'I didn't realise you were having such a rough day.'

Under other circumstances, the thoughtful—even tender—concern in his voice would have made her melt. Now it only infuriated her. 'There are a lot of things you don't realise about me!' she flared.

His eyes narrowed and his body tensed. 'Shauna, what is—'

'Michael, darling!' It was as though Carla had been waiting on the other side of the door, listening for a cue. 'You're back at last!'

Shauna experienced a sickening sense of *déjà vu* as she watched Carla kiss Michael. She clenched her hands as the petite entertainer flirtatiously raised one hand and combed Michael's hair back into order after the embrace.

'I didn't know we had an appointment, Carla,' Michael said evenly.

'We don't,' Carla laughed huskily. 'Although I did tell you I wanted to talk about the show, Friday. I want it to be right—for both of us.' She smiled winsomely. Shauna felt a stab of pure envy. Carla Decker had every female asset in the book, and she knew how to use them. Shauna was aware that even if she had the singer's obvious charms, she'd be unable—and unwilling—to take advantage of them.

Michael smiled briefly. 'I want it to be right, too, babe. And it's all been arranged, remember? You just have to show up and sing.'

Carla tossed her head, her dusky curls bouncing. 'I know, but I do worry.' She ran long, frost-pink nails lightly down his arm. 'Humour me, darling.'

'I generally do,' he responded drily.

'Then see me down to my limo. I left it out front when I arrived.'

'I suppose you expect SEE to pick up the inevitable parking ticket?'

'Umm-hmm,' she agreed, linking arms with him.

'I'll be back shortly, Shauna,' Michael said.

'Yes, sir,' she replied, swivelling her chair back to her typewriter and mechanically threading a clean piece of stationery through the roller. She meticulously re-adjusted the margin stops.

'Bye-bye,' Carla called and walked towards the elevator with Michael, laughing.

Her final two days as Michael's secretary passed in something of a blur. A series of client crises and other business emergencies combined to keep Shauna working at a frantic pace. While Michael responded to the demands of each situation with unfailing energy and creative expertise, his manner towards her veered sharply from curt and cool to almost hostile.

Maybe he just can't accept the fact that for once a woman isn't going to give him what he wants, she thought after he acidly pointed out an error in a letter she'd typed up. The Sebastian male ego can't cope with rejection.

Several times she was on the verge of responding in

kind when he snapped at her, but instinct warned her it would be dangerous. She'd had a taste of his temper that night at the Tempest recording session, and she had no desire to risk exposure to it again.

By the time the end of the week arrived, Shauna was stretched to the limits of her endurance. As Friday drew to a close, she found herself watching the clock with something very near to desperation.

She didn't want it to end this way. But what could she do? She hadn't wanted to begin loving him, either.

'Are you glad it's over, Miss Whitney?'

Shauna was straightening the work area. She'd been aware of him standing in the door to his office, watching her in silence, but she'd said nothing. She could feel his eyes moving over her as she crossed to the desk to make a notation on Dee's appointment calendar.

'It's been very . . . enlightening,' she replied carefully. 'To tell the truth, I don't know how Dee does it.'

'Don't you?'

She glanced at him, puzzled by his tone. 'I—I beg your pardon?' She found herself bracing for some cutting remark.

A strange expression flickered across his face. 'I only meant that you've handled everything very well these past two weeks,' he told her with quiet sincerity.

Her eyes widened and she felt herself flush in reaction to the unexpected compliment. She was shocked by the intensity of the pleasure it gave her. 'Thank you,' she returned. 'I wasn't sure I'd be able to do it.'

'You never know until you try.' He smiled suddenly. The unforced warmth of it made her catch her breath. She wanted to bask in it like a plant in sunlight.

She shook her head in a small, involuntary gesture of denial. Don't, she warned herself.

She was spared the necessity of making some response when the phone rang. 'Excuse me.' She picked it up. 'Michael Sebastian's office,' she said, her voice not quite steady.

'Having a rough day, huh?' a male voice asked without preamble.

'Hallo?'

'Is big brother watching you?'

'Pardon me?' She felt as though her mind had slipped a gear.

There was a familiar laugh from the other end of the line. 'Hey, it's me, Shauna.'

'Jamie?'

'You got it. You sound kind of down. Is somebody giving you a hard time? Do you want to cry on my shoulder about it?'

She had to smile. 'Thank you for the offer, but no. I'm so glad to hear from you!' Out of the corner of her eye, she saw Michael's face tighten. 'I understand the tour is going well.'

'Yeah, it's OK. I swear we've covered most of New England since I saw you, and we've only been on the road two weeks. This is supposed to be the easy part of the schedule.'

'Where are you now?'

'Long Island, New York. For a pair of concerts. I thought I'd get in touch. Didn't Michael tell you I called earlier in the week?'

'He did, but—'

'Maybe he's trying to keep us apart,' Jamie speculated in a mockingly melodramatic tone. 'He probably doesn't want his innocent kid brother to fall victim to your charms.'

Shauna laughed. 'Oh, I can see that happening.'

'Of course, it could be that he doesn't want you falling victim to my charms,' he continued outrageously. 'By the way, what gives with him? He sounded very strange when I talked to him . . . very stirred up about something. He just about bit my head off when I mentioned you.'

Shauna glanced over at Michael. He was staring at her, a grimly sardonic twist to his mouth. His long, powerful fingers were drumming a slow, deliberate rhythm on the taut muscles of his upper thighs. Except for that small movement, he was utterly still.

Their eyes met. The impact of his brilliant green gaze was as tangible as a touch.

My God, she thought with a jolt. He's furious because I'm talking with Jamie! But that's insane—

'Shauna? Are you still there?' Jamie's voice crackled through the wire.

'Yes. Yes, I'm still here,' she said. 'Look, Jamie, Michael's right here, too. Why don't you speak with him?'

'Oh—sure. Fine. Hey, I'm coming into the city tonight after the show. Maybe we could get together tomorrow and you could come out to the concert. Michael's supposed to go, so you could hitch a ride with him.'

'I'll have to see, Jamie,' Shauna said quickly. 'Thank you for the invitation.' She extended the receiver to Michael. He made no move to take it from her. There was a pained, distant look in his eyes as though he was focusing on some inner vision that gave him absolutely no pleasure. 'It's Jamie,' she told him unnecessarily.

He blinked. 'So I gathered,' he ground out. 'I'll take it at my desk. Good night, Shauna.' With that, he pivoted on his heel and walked back into his office, shutting the door behind him.

'Good night,' she repeated softly, more for herself than for him. She waited until she heard him pick up his receiver, then gently replaced the telephone in its cradle.

'What you really meant was goodbye,' she declared to herself that evening, making the statement aloud as she soaked in her bath.

Shauna sighed restlessly, reaching for the soap. She'd come a long way in recognising and admitting her feelings in the past few weeks. A part of her could rejoice in her new openness and ability to respond. Another part longed for the isolated safety of her old inhibitions.

She washed herself slowly, enjoying the gentle stroke of her palms over her body. There was a time when she would have felt guilty about that—and about lolling so indolently in so much hot water. Now she took deliberate pleasure in the luxury of it.

After rinsing off the lather, she stepped out of the bath. She towelled herself dry then applied delicately scented body lotion to her arms and legs. The fragrance of the cream matched the subtle floral scent of the oil she'd used in her bath.

The heat of the water had lent an attractive flush to her fair skin and there was a rosy invitation to the curve of her lips. Glancing into the mirror over the sink, she had the odd feeling she was looking at a stranger.

She'd pinned her hair up into a haphazard knot at the top of her head to keep it dry. Now, studying her reflection, she released it, shaking her head as the chestnut tresses tumbled over her shoulders in gentle waves. The silken weight of it was like a caress on her sensitised skin. For a few seconds, she surrendered to the feel of it, letting herself imagine it *was* a caress . . .

She blinked, stunned by the erotic power of her fantasising. The tautened thrust of her pink-tipped breasts and the quivering ache in her vitals testified to her body's arousal.

Turning away from the woman in the mirror, she took her green quilted bathrobe from its hook on the back of the bathroom door. She donned it hurriedly, knotting the belt around her waist with a decisive jerk. Controlling her trembling fingers, she dragged a brush ruthlessly through her hair, then secured it back in a thick ponytail.

The fresh floral scent of the bath oil and body lotion still clinging to her skin, Shauna then padded into the main room of the apartment. She flicked on her small television and curled up on the sofa, paying scant attention to the local news broadcast that came to life on the screen.

The brassy theme of a popular late night talk-show jerked her back to reality. She reached over to change

the channel when the announcer's voice arrested her
movement with the enthusiastic declaration—

'Also joining us tonight: singing sensation Carla
Decker!'

Shauna's hand fell away from the dial. With an awful
sense of foreboding, she settled back into her seat.

Normally an early riser, Shauna didn't usually stay up
late enough to see this particular programme. Still, she
was vaguely familiar with the way it ran. True to form, it
began with the host delivering a humorous commentary
on the day's events. Next he introduced his first guest,
the macho star of a new television show. After chatting
with him about the perils of being a male sex symbol, the
MC brought on Carla Decker.

She was a scintillating guest in every sense of the
word. Flirtatious and flamboyant, she traded quips with
the host in a dazzlingly assured manner. She also played
up her considerable sex appeal with an elegantly tousled
hairstyle, dramatic make-up, and a glittery tube of a
dress that clung to her curves in a sluice of mauve and
silver beading.

'So, are you ready to do a song for us?' the host asked
finally, drawing applause from the audience.

'Well—' Carla feigned coy reluctance. 'If you really
insist . . .'

Buoyed by still more applause, she got up and strolled
centre stage, accepting a hand microphone from a sound
man.

'Thank you very much,' she said huskily, looking
directly into the camera. 'Because you're all so nice, I'd
like to do something different for you tonight.' She
played out the cord on the microphone in a skilled
movement, twisting it through her fingers. 'This was
written by a very special friend of mine.' She smiled
coquettishly. 'It's the kind of song that gets under your
skin . . . but then, so does he.' She paused as a knowing ripple of laughter swept through the audience. 'I
wanted to sing this the moment I heard it,' she went
on. 'And . . . I always get what I want.'

Shauna went ice cold. She knew what was coming. Even before the band started playing, she knew.

Four measures of introduction. She could see the notes of the melody inked on the white sheets of paper Michael had given her. Those notes were burned into her memory like the words penned beneath them. She wanted to scream with pain at hearing them played out like this.

Then Carla started to sing.

CHAPTER NINE

SOME think for each, there is a lover—
to hold them through the night.

Shauna felt as though a giant hand was gripping her heart, cruelly squeezing the life out of it. Memories, fragments of conversations, came flooding back to her. How could she have been so blind? So stupid?

To keep them safe, and give them comfort,
'til the dark gives way to light.

Carla had wanted the song from the moment she'd heard it and Michael—the man who ran her career and was her lover—had made certain she got what she wanted. What was it she'd said to him that day in the office? Something about wanting this particular appearance to be right for both of them . . .

Until you find the one you're meant for . . .
you go through life apart.

Had Michael even bothered to tell Carla that the words to the song weren't his? Had he simply taken credit for it as he took so many other things in life? Carla had said it was written 'by a special friend'. Or perhaps he'd shared the secret with her and they'd laughed about it the way they'd laughed that day in the lobby.

You are alone. You are an island—
The keeper of an untouched heart.

She hated him! He'd manipulated her . . . used her . . .

seen her vulnerability and turned it to his own advantage. For the first time in her adult life, she'd unlocked the door to her heart to another person. He'd taken her trust and abused it, destroyed it . . . acting with the uncaring malice of a vandal.

And God, she'd been so easy for him! A few carefully dropped references about his childhood had stirred her sympathy and compassion. A few calculated compliments—his music, her words, *their* song—had prompted her to believe that he was attracted to her. And, of course, a handful of mind-drugging, soul-stealing kisses had aroused her long-hidden desires and passion for life. Oh, yes, she'd been a pitifully easy target.

Carla was on the last verse of the song, her sultry voice throbbing sinuously around the lyrics as she gazed squarely into the camera lens. Her eyes were liquid with yearning.

> Some think for each, there is a moment—
> A perfect time. A perfect place.
> When finally, your search is over,
> And at last, you can embrace.
> We'll drink the wine. We'll make the music—

'NO!'

It was more a cry of anguish than a word. The sound came tearing out of Shauna's body, raw and aching, overriding Carla's smoky voice. The singer was giving the words a meaning that she had never meant them to have. It was a hungry, sensual meaning that brought hot, shamed colour into her cheeks as she heard and understood it.

Something inside her snapped. Driven totally by instinct, she stormed into her small bedroom and flung off her robe, tossing it heedlessly on the floor. Hands shaking, she pulled on jeans and a shirt, then quickly thrust her feet into a pair of sneakers. Returning to the other room, she paused long enough to snatch up her handbag and stuff her apartment keys into her pocket before slamming out the door.

It was cold outside, but she didn't feel it. Although her body trembled as she furiously signalled a passing cab, it had nothing to do with the temperature.

She gave the cabbie Michael's address in a taut voice, adding unnecessarily that she was in a great hurry. She sat on the edge of the seat, her fists clenched, staring blindly into space as the taxi took off. She did not see the sharp look the driver gave her in his rear-view mirror. He was clearly uneasy about her pale, set features and stormy eyes.

The doorman at Michael's elegant building was equally wary. Shauna didn't notice. She made her request that he ring Mr Sebastian's apartment with machine-like calm. If Michael wasn't there, she would wait. If he was, she was going to see him.

'Mr Sebastian?' the doorman enquired politely into the house telephone. 'Yes, it's Murphy downstairs in the lobby. There's a Miss Whitney here to see you. She says—' He stopped, obviously being interrupted on the other end. 'Yes, sir, Mr Sebastian. Right away.' He replaced the phone and looked at Shauna. 'Mr Sebastian says you should go right up, Miss Whitney. It's apartment number—'

'I know. Thank you.'

What if he wasn't alone? The possibility struck her as she stepped into the lift and pressed the correct button with an unsteady finger. What if someone's with him?'

She swallowed hard. What difference did it make? He'd already stripped her soul bare for the world to see. She was beyond caring if she had an audience now.

The lift arrived at his floor and the doors slid open. She got out and walked towards Michael's apartment. She raised her hand to knock, half expecting the door to open as she stood there. She rapped once, twice, then froze as she heard Michael's voice, sharp and cutting, coming from the other side. She couldn't make out the words, but the tone was savage.

She knocked again, louder this time. There was still no answer. Heart pounding, she tried the knob. It gave easily. She let herself in, following the sound of Michael's voice into the living room of the apartment.

He was on the telephone, standing with his back to her. The television set was turned on with no sound. It was turned to the talk show Shauna had been viewing. Obviously, Michael had been watching Carla.

From the look of things, he had not been home very long. His suit jacket and tie were draped carelessly over the back of the modular sofa and his shoes had simply been abandoned in the middle of the floor.

She thought later that she must have made some sound, alerting him to her presence. He turned, eyes blazing, his fingers raking back through his thick, dark hair.

'I don't care how, Emmett,' he said, his voice lethally soft. 'Just do it.' He hung up.

Time stopped. For uncounted and agonising moments, they faced each other, motionless and staring. Anger, hurt, and a corrosive sense of betrayal welled up inside Shauna, threatening to overwhelm her.

'Shauna—' Michael took two steps towards her, his green eyes turbulent as they searched her alabaster-white face. He reached forward and caught her shoulder.

The touch was enough to shatter what little control she had lift. How dare he! How dare he speak to her in that gentle, appealing way! He plainly knew why she was there; she could see it in his face. Was he so arrogant —so contemptuous of her—that he believed a little charm was all that was needed to soothe her?

She jerked away, shaking. 'You bastard,' she spat out, her changeable eyes growing glassy and wild. 'You *bastard*! I hate you!'

She hit him, putting the full force of her arm behind the slap. The impact of the blow snapped his head to one side. She felt an awful sense of satisfaction as she saw him wince. At least she'd been able to hurt him back in some small way.

She started to turn, but was pulled back around to face him with such urgency that she dropped her handbag. The fingers that bit into her flesh were iron hard and bruising.

'At least let me explain—'

She gave something perilously close to an hysterical laugh. 'Explain what? That you simply reverted to type? That you wanted something and you got it—any way you could? Oh, I'll give you this. You did warn me what you were—a taker. But I didn't believe that was really true. Do you know why? Because you filled my head with lies—lies!—about how you understood my feelings about my poetry and about that s-song. *Our song!*' She threw the two words at him as though the mere thought of them made her sick. 'I suppose that's what you and Carla call it, too!'

'Damn you, Shauna—' His voice was harsh.

She shook her head, too caught up in her own hurt to see the pain in his face. 'No. Damn you, Michael Sebastian. I *trusted* you! You made me see things—feel things . . . oh, God, why couldn't you just have let me go on the way I was?'

'I could ask you the same question.'

Shauna made a small, choking sound in the back of her throat. 'You could ask me—' she forced out.

'I want to tell you about the song,' he went on imperatively. 'Yours and mine. Not Carla's.'

'Oh, it's Carla's!' She tried to pull free of him, practically screaming the words. 'I heard her sing it tonight. I heard her say it was written by a special friend—a *special friend.*' She repeated the phrase contemptuously. 'I also heard what she made of the song.'

Michael would release her. Aroused, his own temper matched hers, fuelled by sources she could barely dream of. 'She sang my music and your words, Shauna,' he told her sharply. 'And she didn't make anything out of that song that wasn't already there.'

'No.' She denied it in a breathless, horrified voice.

'Yes! You poured your deepest, truest feelings into that poem—and into the others I read. You admitted as much to me. Why can't you admit it to yourself? You're a beautiful, passionate, responsive woman. Yes, your Aunt Margaret did a damned good job of trying to force you into some kind of emotional straight-jacket. But denying your feelings isn't the same thing as not having them. You've got desires and wants, Shauna. I've seen them. Felt them. I know.'

'You don't know anything about me.'

'Don't I?' The naked blaze of emotion in his eyes was enough to make her tremble. 'I know this—'

He pulled her against him, locking them together, making her utterly aware of how the yield and curve of her body complemented the strength and thrust of his. One powerful hand stroked up the fluid line of her back, tracing the sensitive column of her neck. She felt the snap of the rubber band as his fingers tangled ruthlessly in her hair. Freed from their restraint, the chestnut tresses tumbled down in a silken tangle.

Then his mouth covered hers, hungrily taking her lips, exploring the soft sweetness within. It was an act of possession and domination in the first angry moments, as he skilfully and single-mindedly overcame her automatic rebellion. He gentled the kiss, yet deepened his demand, as he felt her first unwilling but unmistakable quiver of response.

'Don't fight me, Shauna. Love, don't—' he breathed, trailing a burning pattern of kisses up the smooth line of her jaw.

'Please—' The appeal came out on a sob. Innocent as she was, she felt the way her body was straining to meet his. She also knew that in this battle, she was fighting herself.

He was wooing her with soft, erotic whispers, but the words made no sense. She was deafened by the drumming of blood in her ears and the primitive pounding of her pulse. She was afraid: afraid he would take her further, afraid he would not. She shuddered as he murmured something unintelligible into her ear and then lightly flicked the lobe with his warm, moist tongue.

His lips moved to reclaim hers once again, this time with a searching, caressing deliberation. At the same moment, he scooped her up in his arms and carried her swiftly over to the couch. Without breaking the kiss, he placed her down, pressing her back against the cream-coloured cushions. Shauna twisted rebelliously, struggling against the seductive lure of the body that moved against and imprisoned her own.

Deftly, he pulled her shirt free from her jeans and slid one hand under the material and up her torso. The heat of his flattened palm seemed to brand her skin as it moved over her, moulding and memorising the exquisite lines of her upper body.

She gasped, arching in shocked awareness, as one hand closed possessively over the swell of one of her breasts. The response of her flesh to the skilled, intimate touch was instantaneous. Shauna felt as though she was being pulled, drowning, into a vortex of liquid fire. She moaned, trying to fight the attraction.

Michael lifted his mouth from hers, drawing a shuddery breath. His features were taut. 'Look at me,' he commanded huskily.

She shook her head, her refusal coming out as a whimper from the back of her throat. If she looked at him, she would be lost. The touch, the taste, the scent of him held her captive. But to see him—

'Shauna, look . . . at . . . me.' The command became a plea—a plea from a man who took rather than asked to be given.

She was lost. Her lids fluttered open to reveal the emotion-clouded depths of her hazel eyes. Helplessly, she stared up into the molten depths of his consuming green gaze.

'I know you,' he said fiercely. 'I think I've known you since the first time I saw you. I ache with it . . . burn with it. But knowing isn't enough. I want you, Shauna. I *need* you. I need your passion and your poetry—'

His voice dropped to a whisper. In her struggles, the top buttons of her shirt had come undone, the fabric parting to display the quivering upper curve of her small breasts. Slowly, reverently, he bent his head and pressed his mouth to the fragrant, shadowed cleft.

The word poetry burned across her already fevered brain like a whip of flame. He wanted . . . dear God, *he wanted* . . .

For a terrible moment, the pain and shock of what she was on the verge of giving in to left her rigid. Then, frantically, she lashed out, pushing at him with a furious and unexpected strength.

Her sudden stillness gave him a little warning, but not enough. The desperation of her struggle caught him off guard enough so that she had a chance to break free of him. She scrambled off the couch, her face deadly pale and her eyes huge and wounded.

'Shauna—' Michael got to his feet, his own expression full of anguish. He was visibly fighting for control.

'Don't touch me!' She was sick with loathing for herself and for him, her slender body going hot and cold by turns. She flinched as he took a step towards her.

The colour drained out of his face, leaving him white beneath his tan. He looked as though he had just received a body blow. 'I don't want to hurt you,' he said.

She lifted one shaking hand to her cheek, only vaguely registering the hot flow of tears that had started to fall from her eyes. 'It's not a matter of what you want, Michael. It's a matter of what you've done. But don't worry—' She blinked here and managed a derisive smile. 'You can't hurt me any more. There's nothing left you can do to me.'

The telephone rang. The sound was shocking in its shrillness.

She saw Michael tense, but his eyes never moved from her face.

'Shauna, please,' he said. 'Don't—'

She shook her head. 'You'd better answer that,' she

said in a flat little voice. 'Maybe it's Carla Decker. If it is, you can tell her she can have the song . . . my poem. I don't care about it. Not now.'

At that, her control broke and she turned and ran, finding her way out of the apartment on pure panicked instinct. Bypassing the lift, she dashed for the stairwell, racing as though her life depended on it.

That she made it down more than a dozen flights without stumbling was a miracle. She was too blinded by tears to see properly and too uncaring to take any precautions. In a way, she would have welcomed a fall. Physical pain would have been nothing compared with the emotional agony she was experiencing.

She scarcely checked her headlong pace as she came out of the stairwell and into the plush lobby area. She brushed by a well-dressed, middle-aged couple standing by the bank of lifts, not caring that they regarded her dishevelled appearance with undisguised shock.

'Miss Whitney, please—' The uniformed attendant who had admitted her earlier reached out a detaining hand as she got to the door. He was holding the house telephone in the other. 'Mr Sebastian—miss, please!'

She darted past him, out the door, and into the night.

She ran. The direction and the distance didn't matter. She ran until she couldn't run any more and then, gasping for breath, she spotted an empty cab waiting at a red light.

She reached it only a few seconds before the light changed. Wrenching open the back door, she slid in.

'Hey, what the—' the driver exclaimed, turning around. His surprise turned to concerned alarm as he got a good look at Shauna. 'Lady, are you OK?'

'Yes,' she managed to get out, making a futile attempt to wipe the tears off her face. Glancing down distractedly, she saw that her blouse was still partially unbuttoned. She made an equally futile attempt to do it up.

'Lady, you look like you need a policeman or a doctor.'

'No,' She shook her head. 'I'm just—I need to go home. P-please.'

The light had changed by this time. The car behind them sounded its horn in an impatient blast.

The cabbie swore.

'Please,' Shauna repeated, terrified the man might order her out of his vehicle.

The driver said something under his breath as he shifted back and lifted his foot off the brake. 'Tell me where I'm going,' he instructed gruffly. 'But I still think you'd be better off if I took you to a precinct house or a hospital.'

It wasn't until the cab pulled up in front of her apartment that Shauna realised she'd left her handbag in Michael's apartment. Her panic-stricken eyes met the driver's wearily comprehending ones in the rear-view mirror.

To her surprise, the man turned around and slid open the Plexiglass partition that separated him from his passengers. She was even more startled when he extended a handful of tissues.

'Let me guess. No money, right?'

Her fingers trembling, Shauna took the tissues and used them. Struggling for some semblance of control, she drew a shuddery breath and made a choked sound half-way between a sob and a hiccough. It had been a long, long time since she'd cried.

'I'm sorry,' she told him through unsteady lips. 'My bag . . . I left it—I—I have some money in my apartment if you c-can wait—'

The driver, whose homely face had a very lived-in look, shook his head. 'Nah,' he rasped. 'To tell you the truth, I didn't throw the meter anyway. Call it my good deed for the night.'

'But—' This unexpected act of kindness threatened to bring more tears.

'Hey, now, don't start crying again! It's OK, lady. Whatever it is. You're home now, right? Just like you wanted. Now, is there somebody to let you in?'

'Let me in?'

'Uh-huh. If you don't have your bag, you're probably locked out.'

'I'm afraid—' Suddenly, she remembered sticking her keys into her jeans' pocket. 'No, wait—' Twisting, she fished them out. 'I didn't put them in my bag,' she explained needlessly, gesturing with them.

'OK.' The man nodded. 'Are you really sure you don't want any help—'

'No. I'm going to b-be all right.'

'Nothing's ever as bad as it seems.' This unoriginal bit of philosophy was dispensed in a comforting tone. 'Now, I'll watch until you get inside.'

'Thank you. I—I appreciate it. You've been very kind.'

The man shrugged a little, possibly embarrassed by his own burst of good Samaritanism. 'Good night, lady,' he said.

The phone was ringing when Shauna unlocked the door to her apartment. It was an angry, demanding sound. She knew who was on the other end. She let it go on ringing, gritting her teeth against the noise.

She'd left the lights on and the television playing when she'd run out. Walking over to the set, she clicked it off in an abrupt gesture.

The phone stopped ringing.

She walked into her bedroom like a zombie and stripped off her clothes, dropping them in an unwanted pile on the floor. She retrieved the robe she had discarded so hurriedly and put it on, wrapping it around herself like a security blanket.

The face that looked back at her from the bathroom mirror was white. She spent a few moments splashing cold water on her skin in a vain effort to bring some colour back into her pale cheeks.

'I'm going to be all right,' she whispered to her reflection. The words sounded even hollower now than they had when she'd said them to the cab driver. The haunted, anguished expression in her clouded eyes and the bruised softness of her mouth told the real story.

Combing her fingers through the tangles of her hair, she wandered back into the main room of her apartment. Staring dazedly around, she saw that she had neglected to properly lock the front door. With a bitter smile twisting her lips, she rectified her mistake.

'It's l-like locking the b-barn door after the horse has escaped,' she told herself with a helpless, unsteady laugh that turned into a sob. Sucking in her breath, she dug her nails into her palms, willing herself not to start weeping again.

Blindly, she walked over to the sofa and sat down, curling up in the corner. Her posture was wary and withdrawn.

What had he done to her? What had she *let* him do? Even while her mind knew Michael Sebastian for a liar, a user, and a cheat . . . her body had responded to his. There had been a few moments—suspended between the anger and the fear—when she had wanted him just as much as he wanted her.

I want you, Shauna. I need you. I need your passion and your poetry—

She put her hands over her ears, trying to block out the searing memory of those words. But there was nothing she could do to stop the hot wave of physical remembrance that swept over her. She could still feel the heated, hungry tenderness of Michael's searching lips and fingers on her naked sensitised skin.

'Shauna! Damn you, answer me!'

She froze like a terrified animal trapped in the headlights of an on-rushing car. For a few moments, she forgot how to breathe.

Michael? Here?

'Go away,' she said in a tiny, shattered voice.

'Shauna, please!' The two words were punctuated by what sounded like a clench-fisted blow to the door. Her eyes dropped as she heard the rattle of the knob.

Somehow, she got to the door.

'Shauna? If you're in there, just say something.'

She was trembling violently. 'I'm in here.'

There was a long silence from the other side. Part of her wished desperately for a peephole in the door so she could look out into the hallway; the other part felt a kind of demented gratitude that she couldn't see him. She wasn't at all certain of what she would do if she did.

'Thank God.' There was a thudding noise as though he'd leaned against the door. 'Are you—all right?' The question was low and strained.

'Go away and leave me alone.'

'Just tell me you're all right.'

'I'm all right,' she replied bitterly, blinking hard against the hot flow of tears welling up in her eyes. 'As if you cared.'

There was another long silence. When Michael spoke again, his voice was clear and utterly controlled.

'I'm leaving your bag, Shauna,' he said. 'I don't expect you to open the door while I'm still here. I'll go away and leave you alone after I've said two things. First, I did not give the song—our song—to Carla Decker. Second, I do . . . care.' She had to strain to hear him. 'I care very much.'

'Shauna, snap out of it!'

Shauna was sitting at her desk, lost in an emotional fog. She'd taken off her gloves and hat, but she was still wearing her coat.

I care very much.

Those four simple words had possessed her, obsessed her, throughout the entire weekend . . . twisting her heart with hurt one moment and stirring it with insane hopes the next.

Why had he said it? And why had she heard so much tension, so much hesitation, in the way he'd spoken? It had been as though he'd found the words unfamiliar and difficult to say.

Were they difficult for him to say because they were a

lie? Yet if he were the deceiver and manipulator she'd accused him of being, why would he have trouble with a four-word falsehood?

Or were they difficult for him to say because they were the truth. Oh, God, what if they were?

I want . . . I need . . . I care . . .

Michael Sebastian had said all three things to her. He had not said *I love*.

Neither had she. But she had, out of anger, hurt pride and jealousy, told him she *hated*.

Supposing he did care? Would that change what he had done to her?

What she *thought* he'd done to her. What if he'd been telling the truth as he stood outside her apartment door?

'Shauna, are you all right?'

She started violently, her heart racing. She glanced around wildly, suddenly aware of where she was and what she had been doing—or not doing.

'What is the matter with you?' The question came from one of the Legal Department's other secretaries. She and one of SEE's junior lawyers were standing by Shauna's desk, their expressions fluctuating between impatient irritation and bewildered concern.

'S-sorry,' Shauna apologised unsteadily. She rose and pulled off her coat. 'I—I had a rough weekend.'

The lawyer—the same one who'd tried to date her after news of her temporary position with Michael Sebastian had become known—made a face. 'Well, get ready for a rough week,' he counselled.

'I beg your pardon?' Shauna sat back down, smoothing her hair in an unthinking gesture. She'd worn it pulled back off her forehead in front and loose and flowing at the back.

'You don't have to be discreet,' Elaine, the secretary, said. 'Everyone knows. It's in the papers.'

'I don't understand—'

'Carla Decker,' the lawyer said. 'Come on, Shauna. This can't have been the totally unexpected bombshell the press is trying to make out. You've been up with Michael Sebastian for the past two weeks. Do you honestly think we'll believe you didn't have some inkling?'

'Some inkling of what?' She was astonished she could get the question out at all, much less ask it with such quiet steadiness. Carla Decker . . . Carla Decker . . . the name was like a knife into her soul.

Elaine rolled her eyes. 'Her contract with SEE has been ripped up!'

'*What?*' Shauna felt the blood drain out of her face. For a moment, she thought she was going to faint.

'My—you really didn't know,' the young lawyer said in a tone of amazed discovery.

'What—what happened?'

'That's what we're trying to find out,' Elaine told her crossly. 'All we know so far is that Michael Sebastian personally dropped the axe on the Divine Decker over the weekend. One of the trade paper columnists say it happened while she was doing that network talk show Friday night. Something about artistic differences over a song. But that doesn't make any sense—'

'There's Mr Barkley,' the lawyer interrupted urgently. 'We'd better get back to work, ladies.' He moved away while Elaine darted back to her desk.

'Good morning, Shauna,' Emmett Barkley said as he walked by. Although his tone was politely pleasant, there was a grim element to his usual dignity.

'Good morning, Mr Barkley,' she responded, keeping her gaze carefully fixed on her desk top.

Artistic differences over a song. Elaine was right: it *didn't* make any sense. Unless . . .

Shauna closed her eyes, feeling as though the ground had dropped out from beneath her feet. 'Oh, God,' she whispered in a stricken voice as the explanation came to her.

There had been a copy of the lead sheets for their song in Michael's desk upstairs. Carla had had access to it that day she'd dropped in unexpectedly. She'd been in

Michael's office alone, behind a closed door, for more than an hour.

It all fitted together with sickening neatness. Filled with shame and remorse, Shauna writhed inwardly as she reflected on what she had done. And the things she had accused Michael of! Perhaps there had been some small justification for her initial reaction, but there had been no excuse for her refusal to listen to his side of the story. She'd been so caught up in her own overwhelming sense of hurt that she'd ignored everything but the desire to hurt in return.

And yet . . . and yet, Michael had come after her. He'd come after her to deny, in one simple sentence, that he had done what she believed him guilty of. He'd also come after her to say he cared . . . very much.

Slowly, Shauna reached for the phone on her desk. Picking up the receiver, she dialled an extension she now knew by heart.

'Michael Sebastian's office.'

'Hello—Dee? This is Shauna Whitney. I—welcome back.'

There was a wry chuckle from the other end. 'It's sweet of you to call, Shauna. To tell the truth, if I'd known what kind of mess I was returning to, I would have stayed away much longer!'

'You mean . . . Carla Decker?'

'Exactly. Just between the two of us, I'd had the feeling the Divine Decker had been turning Michael more off than on for the past few months, but I never expected such a dramatic break-up. The phone has been ringing off the hook since I got in.'

'It must be a madhouse,' Shauna sympathised. She took a deep breath, steeling herself. 'Is—is Michael there?'

'Don't I wish!' Dee returned feelingly. 'There was a message waiting for me first thing this morning. He's out. Period. I had to cancel about a dozen appointments.'

Shauna's heart plunged. 'Do you know where he is?' she asked quickly.

'No. And I don't think anybody else does, either. Jamie Cord's called twice trying to locate him. He wanted to know if Michael's coming to Tempest's recording session tonight. I told him it's still on the calendar. But who knows with this Carla Decker situation—oh, damn! There goes another line. Look, Shauna, is there something you want me to tell Michael—'

'No, no. Thank you, Dee. It's something I have to—to take care of myself.'

'Well, all right. By the way, you left everything in wonderful order up here. The office hasn't been this organised in ages! I hope the two weeks weren't too hard on you. Now, I've really got to go.'

'Goodbye,' Shauna said softly, even though the other woman had already disconnected. She hung up the receiver gently, her thoughts fixed on what she knew she must do.

CHAPTER TEN

SHAUNA had been arguing with the lobby guard for nearly five minutes. She stared at him now from behind her glasses, her pale features taut with a mixture of desperation and determination.

'I have to see Mr Sebastian,' she repeated, struggling to keep her voice steady. At least the man had confirmed that Michael Sebastian was in the building for the Tempest recording session.

'Miss, I'm sorry, but I have my orders. I can't let any unauthorised people up.'

'Please!' She was pleading. 'This is very important.'

The guard frowned, possibly taking into account the fact that she neither looked—nor acted—like the groupie type. 'Look,' he said slowly, 'I suppose I could call upstairs. They've broken for dinner or something—'

'No!' Shauna shook her head vehemently. She was afraid that if he called upstairs, Michael would refuse to see her. 'I appreciate your offer, but—' She stopped abruptly as one of the lifts near the guard's desk hissed open. 'Jamie!' she exclaimed, recognising the passenger who got out. She moved to him quickly.

'Shauna?' he looked surprised but pleased to see her. Yet there was an air of disgruntled weariness about him as he stood there, slouching a little, his hands jammed into the pockets of his leather jacket. 'Why are you here?' he asked. His eyes moved over curiously, and she thought she detected a strange flicker as he registered the fact that she was once again wearing her glasses and had her hair pulled back into a demure bun.

'I—I'm here to see Michael,' she explained. 'He *is* here, isn't he?'

Jamie nodded. 'Yeah. The rest of the guys took a

176

dinner break about twenty minutes ago. We weren't accomplishing anything, so it seemed like a smart idea. I stayed behind to talk to Michael. Not so smart. He just about threw me out of the studio.'

She bit her lip. 'What—what's wrong?'

Jamie grimaced. 'Who knows for sure? Michael's always played it close to the chest . . . never really letting anybody get inside his guard. I think whatever's the matter with him now must have something to do with this Carla Decker mess. But what I can't figure out is why he's so worked up over her doing one of his songs. It's not as though he hasn't written numbers for her before.'

'Actually—' Shauna hesitated for a long moment, the beginnings of a blush staining her cheeks. 'Actually, Michael didn't write the song Carla sang.'

'What?' The word exploded out of Jamie. 'Shauna, come on. Michael used to play that tune for me when I first came to live with him after I got out of the rehabilitation programme!'

'He wrote the music,' she amended. 'But . . . the words . . . I—I wrote them.'

'*You* did?' Jamie stared at her.

She nodded.

He whistled, clearly taken aback. 'I only caught the last verse or so on Friday night. One of the roadies had a battery-powered television backstage and was watching Carla do her thing. I recognised the music right off, of course. But the words—they're yours? Really?'

'Really.'

'But you never said anything about writing lyrics—'

She gave a rueful smile. 'I thought I was writing poetry,' she confessed. 'Michael was the one who decided I was a lyricist.'

'But how did he get hold of—' Jamie's puzzled expression changed abruptly, his eyes widening in speculation. 'The envelope you threw at him during the recording session!' he guessed. 'I thought his reaction was sort of strange when he opened it up. Of course, his reaction when he got that first good look at you was sort of strange, too. In fact—'

'Jamie—' She could practically see his mind working.

He looked her straight in the eye. 'You and Michael had some kind of fight about the song, didn't you?' It wasn't really a question.

'Yes,' she said. 'I . . . I accused Michael of giving it to Carla without my permission.'

'Oh.' The single syllable was freighted with a wealth of feeling.

'I'm afraid he hates me after what I said,' she told him painfully, anguish stark on her face.

'Are you crazy?' Jamie was thunderstruck. 'Hey, look, whatever hot and heavy emotions you've stirred up in Michael—and it's pretty obvious you've stirred up a bunch, considering the way he's been acting—hate is not one of them. Hate he could handle. But what he feels for you . . . no wonder he's been behaving like he's gone off the deep end. He has.' He seemed peculiarly pleased.

'I don't—'

'And you're not exactly indifferent to him, either, are you, Shauna?'

She wasn't sure whether she should laugh or cry at this question. Indifferent to Michael Sebastian? She was in love with him! Even when she'd believed he'd betrayed her and abused her trust, she'd responded to him. She'd wanted his kisses, his touch . . . and more.

'No,' she said with a heart-rending smile. 'I'm not exactly indifferent to him. That's why . . . I came here to talk to him.'

'So, talk to him!' Jamie urged instantly.

She glanced over at the guard. Although he was busying himself with his work, she had the feeling he'd been listening to their conversation. 'I wasn't authorised—' she began.

Jamie caught on immediately. 'Got you,' he said, then raised his voice pleasantly. 'Uh—Fred, isn't it?'

The guard looked up. 'Yes, Mr Cord?'

'Fred, I know everybody appreciates how careful you
are about letting people in and out of this place, but Miss
Whitney here is a personal friend of mine and she does
have to see Mr Sebastian. I'm going to escort her
upstairs.'

'Sure thing,' the man nodded. 'Sorry if you were
inconvenienced, miss.'

'Come on,' Jamie said.

They rode up to the third floor in silence. Shauna
twisted the belt of her wrap coat nervously with one
hand. Reaching up with the other, she gave her neatly
styled hair a reassuring pat. Glancing over at Jamie, she
saw his mouth curve into a mysteriously satisfied smile.

The lift came to a stop and the door slid open. Jamie
hit the hold button with his thumb and looked at her. She
was startled by the affectionate understanding she saw in
his face.

'Will you tell me one thing?' he asked, tilting his head
quizzically.

'What?'

'Up in Hartford. Did Michael really wake you up by
turning on the light?'

She flushed but managed to meet his gaze. 'He—
Michael didn't turn on the light when he came in. He just
got undressed and got into bed . . . with me. It was a
very b-big bed and neither of us realised we were
sleeping together until much later.' She gave a small
laugh. '*That's* when he turned on the light. But we
didn't—I haven't—He . . . he did spent the rest of the
night in the other room of the suite,' she finished lamely.

'Yeah, I thought I detected more than a hint of
frustration the next morning,' Jamie answered outrageously. Shauna thought he looked like the proverbial
canary-eating cat. 'It's going to be fine, Shauna. Believe
me.'

She took a deep breath. 'I'm not sure what to say,' she
admitted.

He smiled warmly. 'The lady who wrote the lyrics for
Michael's music won't have any problem finding the

right words,' he told her. 'It's the same studio as before. Ignore the "Keep Out" sign.'

Once out of the lift, she didn't look back. Following the path she had taken so fatefully once before, she walked along the corridor to the studio. The tap-tap of her boot heels on the floor held equal parts of eagerness and anxiety.

There was a horrible moment when she pushed open the door to the control room and realised it was empty. Stomach knotting, she glanced around. He was gone! Somehow, he'd left—

But no. Looking through the glassed front of the control booth, she saw him. The lights in the studio had been dimmed, and Michael was sitting, partially in shadow, at Griz's keyboard. His head was bent and he was picking out notes, apparently at random, with one finger.

Trembling a little, she opened the door that went from the control room to the studio and walked through.

She never knew what alerted him to her presence. Her heart was pounding so thunderously that she thought he might have heard it as she approached him. When she was about ten feet away, he looked up suddenly.

They confronted each other for a long moment, an emotional minefield stretching between them. Shauna felt Michael's green eyes go over her ardently.

'Michael.' She barely breathed his name aloud. He looked awful. There were lines of strain around his mouth and his lean features were rigidly schooled. His body had gone taut as though preparing for an attack.

'What the hell are you doing here?' he asked, very softly. There was none of the angry challenge there had been the first time he'd put that question to her. There was pain, however, and a sense that he didn't quite trust what he was seeing.

Shauna moistened her lips. 'I—I know about the song,' she said. 'I know you didn't give it to Carla D-Decker. I think she must have taken the lead sheets out of your desk that day she was in your office alone.

The things I said to you the other night . . . I was angry
and hurt . . . and j-jealous.' She saw something flare
deep in his eyes for a split-second before it was ruthlessly
extinguished. 'I'm sorry. I—I should have trusted
you.'

'Why? I never gave you any reason to trust me.'

'Yes, you did!' she protested, the words tumbling out.
'You tried to help me—understand me. You . . . shared
things with me.'

'I didn't share enough,' he said. 'I've spent so damn
much of my life keeping people at arm's length, never
letting anybody get close enough to betray me the way
my mother—' He broke off. She watched his strong-
fingered hands clench into fists. The torment she felt
radiating from him tore at her heart. She wanted to
move to him, to comfort him, but she wasn't certain he'd
accept that from her—not now.

'You broke Carla's contract, didn't you?'

'I wish I could have broken her neck!'

The brutality in his voice shook her. 'It's going to
mean a big loss for SEE . . .' she commented hesitantly.

'Considering what Carla's cost me personally, any
price I have to pay to be rid of her professionally will be a
cheap one.' He expelled a long, sighing breath. 'Shauna,
I think you'd better go.' His voice was strained.

'You—you want me to go?' She barely got the question out.

He looked at her. For the first time, his defences were
totally down. There was raw, undisguised emotion—
naked vulnerability—in his eyes.

'No,' he said, 'I don't want you to go. But I don't want
to hurt you any more than I already have, either. And if
you stay—'

'You haven't hurt me, Michael.'

'Haven't I? Look at yourself, Shauna!'

She smiled a little, realising he meant her return to the
staid, touch-me-not hairstyle and the defensive glasses.
'I have,' she replied simply. 'But now I want you to look
at me. This is how I was before we met . . . before you

made me understand what I was doing to my life, and why. I don't want to be this way any more. So—'

She took a deep breath, praying that what she was about to do would convince him of her feelings. Slowly she removed her glasses. After a moment's hesitation she deliberately dropped them on the floor. Her hair came next. She unpinned it with unsteady fingers and shook it loose. Finally, she undid her coat and took it off, letting it slip to the floor. She was wearing the same rust dress she had put on a week before in hopes of pleasing him.

Michael rose, lithe and commandingly male. He said nothing.

'I . . . don't want to be "Miss Whitney",' Shauna told him, struggling to hang on to the remaining shreds of her courage. 'Please, Michael . . .'

'Are you asking me to forget my rule about Mondays?' he asked quietly. His tone gave away nothing, and he was standing far enough away so she couldn't accurately read his expression without her glasses.

Shauna coloured, veiling her eyes with her lashes. She had hoped . . . wished . . . for more. But if this was all he was prepared to give, she loved him too much to turn away from it.

'Yes,' she whispered.

She watched him walk towards her then, with silent, predatory tread. Her body burned with a blood-heating physical awarness of him.

He came to a halt perhaps a foot away from her—near enough so she could smell the distinctively masculine scent of him; near enough so she could reach out and touch him.

'I don't want to seduce you, Shauna,' he said. There was an aching tenderness in the way he pronounced her name. 'What I want to do—what I've wanted to do practically from the first moment I saw you—is to love you . . . to cherish you—'

Then she was in his arms, and he was holding her, moulding her against him as though they were two halves of a perfect whole. Trusting her instincts, Shauna melted into the embrace, surrendering to his strength. In a wordless movement of supplication, she tilted her head up. Michael would never have to take from her; she would freely give him everything he wanted.

For a heart stopping moment, he seemed to hold back. Her eyes huge and melting with love, Shauna reached up and touched the lean plane of one of his tanned cheeks. Her lips parted as she felt a tremor of reaction run through him. Emboldened by his response, she lifted her hand higher and brushed back the lock of dark hair that had once again curved down over his forehead.

He kissed her, gently, almost reverently. She answered him with a yearning eagerness, opening her lips to him. He deepened the kiss, drinking in her sweetness with the compelling need of a thirsty man who has gone too long without the taste of fresh water. Shauna's arms swept up, locking around his neck. The unconscious movements of her slender body were untutored but unmistakably arousing. She was aware of the press of her soft breasts against the hard wall of his chest and of the strain of her thighs against his.

There was a wild, wanton beauty in her delicate features when he finally broke free of the embrace and put her away from him. He took a deep gulp of air, breathing like a distance runner at the end of a marathon race.

'Michael—' Shauna asked dazedly.

'You've got to help me,' he said. 'We have to talk, Shauna . . . before we go any further. Afterwards—' She saw the heat of desire flare in his eyes, turning the gold glints there molten. His gaze moved over her in frank hunger, marking her femininity and claiming it for his own. 'Afterwards, if there's going to be a first time for us, I want it to be right. The perfect time . . . the perfect place.'

She didn't even realise that he was quoting her own words at her. Only one word registered, slicing into her consciousness like a deadly shard of glass. '"If"?' she asked. Such a small word. So little, but so painful.

'I think I fell in love with you the moment I saw you for the first time,' he said. 'But I was too blind to realise what had happened to me. Love wasn't—isn't—an emotion I have much familiarity with. I saw what loving a woman did to my father and I decided that wasn't for me. Then, growing up the way I did, making a career in this business . . . there were women. I used them. They used me. And love was just a word I put in my songs. Until you.'

The rawness of his confession moved her deeply. He spoke awkwardly, with none of the verbal ease she had seen him demonstrate over and over again during their two weeks of working together.

'Michael—' she said, touching his arm. 'It doesn't matter. You don't have to explain—'

His hand closed over hers, his clasp warmly possessive. 'But I do. When I said I fell in love with you the first time I saw you, I didn't mean here in the studio. I was talking about that scene at the elevator.'

She opened her mouth to say something. He silenced her gently, pressing a finger to her lips.

'Carla Decker and I had an on-off affair for several years. I never wanted to get seriously involved with anyone, but I am a man . . . with a man's physical needs. Carla was there. She didn't want to get involved, either. The only two things she's ever cared about are herself and her career. Having an affair with me—appearing to have one, in recent months—was useful to her.' He paused, watching her face searchingly. 'Shauna, it's not a relationship I'm proud of. Especially not since you were hurt by it. That day you caught the two of us on the elevator was the day I saw just how empty and meaningless things were between Carla and me. How empty and meaningless so much of my life was.'

'I—I don't understand.'

'The look on your innocent, beautiful face stopped me cold. I made the remark about outraged virtue because I didn't want to admit what you made me feel about myself.' He hesitated, obviously choosing his words with care. 'I haven't touched Carla—or any other woman —since that day. And if you're wondering about finding her at my apartment, don't. She was only there because there'd been some mix-up in her hotel reservation and she invited herself to stay. I have two spare bedrooms. She slept in one of them, alone.' His lips twisted into a brief smile. 'Carla's a talented, thoughtless bitch, but she's got infallible instincts when it comes to protecting her own interests. I think the reason she came on so strong that morning, and on the other occasions when you saw her, was because she recognised that you were something very special. And I . . . I was do damned confused about my feelings—'

'*You* were confused?' Shauna exclaimed. 'I never knew what to think from one moment to the next!'

He stroked her silky hair in a tender movement. 'I was afraid,' he admitted. 'I wanted you badly, but I knew simply taking you to bed wasn't going to be enough. I was jealous—God, I wanted to strangle Jamie for the way you smiled at him! And that day you were late to the office . . . I was terrified I'd never see you again. Even once I had the guts to accept the attraction was more than physical, I still tried to fool myself. I tried to tell myself the reason I kept hammering at the psychological fortress you'd barricaded yourself behind was that I couldn't bear to see someone with your warmth and talent lock herself away. The truth was—the truth is—I can't stand the sense of being closed out.' Michael cupped her face in his palms.

Shauna realised she had been holding her breath. She let it out slowly. 'You're not closed out,' she told him, her hazel eyes shimmering. 'I love you.' There! She'd finally said it!

'Oh, God . . . you don't know what it means to me to hear you say that,' he said thickly.

'As much as it would mean to me to hear you say it.'

'I do love you, my darling,' he told her fervently, the

melting adoration in his eyes echoing and underlining the declaration in compelling fashion. 'The music I wrote—that I used with your poetry—I always knew it was incomplete. Melody but no meaning. My song without words. But you've given me the words—the meaning . . .'

His arms slipped around her, protective and possessive at the same time. Shauna gloried in the embrace, feeling her heart expand with happiness. She stared up at his lean-featured, handsome face, seeing the look of love with the eyes of love. The true measure of what he felt for her was that he'd opened the doors of his own psychological fortresses . . . hammered down the barriers of caution and mistrust so they could reach each other without restraint.

'Tell me what you want, Mr Sebastian,' she urged in a softly provocative voice. She could feel the virile thrust of his desire. The heady knowledge that she was the one who was arousing it sent a wave of pleasure washing over her.

A slow smile curved his lips as he frankly conceded her power over him. 'What do I want? I want to make music with you.' He pressed a kiss to one corner of her waiting mouth. 'I want to make love with you.' He favoured the other corner. 'And—' he teased the soft pink curve of her lower lip with the tip of his tongue. Their breaths mingled intimately. 'And, I want to make a life with you.'

'A life?' Her knees started to buckle as the implications of this comment hit her. His hands tightened on her hips.

Michael made a sound of affirmation, deep in his throat. 'You said you didn't want to be "Miss Whitney",' he said. 'How would you feel about being Mrs Michael Sebastian?'

She managed to pull away from him for an instant. 'You're asking me to marry you?'

'Only if you're going to say yes. Otherwise, I'm telling you.' His manner turned masterful.

'But—'

'We can have Jamie make the room arrangements for the honeymoon,' he went on, playing his fingers caressingly up her back, his heated touch burning through the clinging jersey fabric. 'Although he'll have to make sure we've got a smaller bed than the one up in Hartford. I don't ever want to spend another night sleeping with you, my passionate little poetess, without realising it.'

'Michael!' He was kissing her again, rousing every fibre of her body to flushed, excited life.

'You'll put on those damned glasses of yours so I can take them off again. And pin up this lovely hair of yours so I can let it down,' he continued huskily, sending erotic shivers up and down her spine and stirring her to the very core. 'And then you'll cover nearly every exquisite inch of you in that virginal incitement to seduction you call a nightgown, and I'll give both of us the pleasure of very, very slowly removing—'

'Yes!' she burst out breathlessly, her heart full to overflowing. 'Yes!'

'Yes to what?' he demanded, suddenly fierce.

'To everything.'

'So, what do you think?' Michael asked, lifting his hands off the keys of the piano. He rose with effortless ease, stretching with the lazy grace of a jungle cat. Clad in nothing but a pair of faded jeans, he exuded a potently virile appeal. 'Shauna?'

Curled contentedly in the corner of the modular sofa, Shauna Whitney Sebastian smiled over at her husband. There was more than a hint of invitation in the languid way she shifted her robe-clad body and slowly combed her fingers through her tumble of chestnut hair.

They'd been married nearly a month, and the rightness of it took her breath away. The notion of a 'perfect time' now held a promise of forever in it, and the 'perfect place' was wherever they could be together. By trusting and loving, they were creating a harmony that went far beyond physical intimacy.

'Shauna?' Michael repeated, his voice husky and amused as he walked to where she was seated. The quirk of his brows and the sudden gleam in his eyes told her he was attuned to her mood.

'It's a beautiful piece of music,' she said honestly.

He sat down beside her, gathering her close. 'I had some beautiful inspiration,' he told her, nuzzling gently at the sensitive curve of her jaw.

'Ummm . . .' she breathed, her slender fingers drifting caressingly over the muscled warmth of his naked torso. 'And . . . am . . . I going to be . . . inspired . . . when it comes to the lyrics?'

He sought and found her mouth. The kiss—deeply passionate but carefully controlled—was a long and lingering one.

'Are you inspired, my love?' Michael asked softly after he lifted his dark head, his green eyes noting the sweet parting of her lips and the rosy flush of pleasure on her cheeks.

'What do you think?' She brushed her fingertips lightly through his crisp mat of chest hair.

'I think "Miss Whitney" would be very shocked if she could see us now.' He captured her hand. Lifting it to his mouth, he pressed a kiss to her palm.

Shauna shook her head. 'No, she'd be jealous.' She cuddled against him with a blissful sigh.

At Michael's insistence, they had waited until their wedding night to make love the first time. He'd been tender with her innocence, easing her instinctive fears and holding his own experienced desires in careful check. With loving expertise, he'd guided her beyond fantasies and poetic imaginings and initiated her into a world of intensely pleasurable realities.

Michael slipped one hand underneath the fold of her robe, cupping her breast. Her breathing quickened as she felt his thumb stroke teasingly over the nipple, rousing it to taut, quivering responsiveness.

'Didn't you say something earlier about wanting to watch Tempest's appearance on *Saturday Show* tonight?' he asked her in a deceptively innocent voice.

She caught her breath. 'I totally forgot!' she exclaimed. 'Is it too late?'

'Hit the remote control for the television set and see,' he counselled indulgently.

Shauna did as he advised, sighing with relief when she saw the programme was still on. The *Saturday Show*'s resident comedy troupe was in the middle of a droll parody of a popular television series.

'You don't supposed we missed it?' she asked, giving him an anxious look.

Michael shook his head. 'This show is usually designed to close with a musical number,' he said knowledgeably. 'But if we did miss it, I'm sure Tempest will give us a private performance. After all, sweetheart, it's *our* song.'

She laughed happily at this and snuggled against him. 'I like the sound of that,' she commented.

'Let's hope you like the sound of the arrangement, too.'

'I'm sure I—oh, here they are!'

The announcer's introduction was short and the welcoming applause from the studio audience was loudly enthusiastic. As the applause died down, Jamie stepped forward to the microphone, grinning boyishly.

'Thank you,' he said conversationally. 'We'd like to do a brand new song for you now. It was written by two people Tempest cares a lot about . . . they care a lot about each other, too. I think once you hear this number, you'll know these two have something special together. This is for Shauna and Michael.'

There were four measures of introduction, played with elegant, almost classical, simplicity by Griz at the keyboard and counterpointed by a smooth progression of chords from Hank and Frank's guitars. Shauna could see the notes of the melody inked on the white sheets of paper Michael had given her. Those notes were engraved on her heart and mind like the words penned beneath them.

Jamie started to sing.

> Some think for each, there is a lover—
> to hold them through the night.
> To keep them safe, and give them comfort,
> 'til the dark gives way to light.
> Until you find the one you're meant for . . .
>   you go through life apart . . .

Shauna pressed the remote control switch, shutting the television off. Her eyes were misty with emotion.

'Shauna?' Michael asked softly.

She looked at him for a long moment, drinking in his dark male strength. 'I'm glad we gave the song to Tempest,' she said, 'but I don't need to hear the whole thing to know how right it is. Besides, I know how it ends . . . I love you, Michael.'

She could see her own feelings reflected in his expressive face. 'That, my darling, is how it begins,' he replied, standing up. 'Come to bed.'

They walked from the room hand in hand, fingers intertwined with an intimacy their bodies would soon repeat. As they reached the end of the hallway that led to their bedroom, Michael swept Shauna up into his arms, cradling her against his bared chest.

'My love,' he said with tender simplicity.

Shauna smiled with eager radiance. Then, lifting her arm, pulled his head down for a kiss, full of the joyful knowledge that she had found the one she was meant for . . . and so had he.